Mister Tidwell, Gunner

A full list of L. Ron Hubbard's
novellas and short stories is provided at the back.

*Dekalogy—a group of ten volumes

L. RON HUBBARD

Mister Tidwell, Gunner

GALAXY
PRESS

Published by
Galaxy Press, LLC
7051 Hollywood Boulevard, Suite 200
Hollywood, CA 90028

Printed in the United States of America.

ISBN-10 1-59212-397-X
ISBN-13 978-1-59212-397-1

Library of Congress Control Number: 2007927525

Contents

Stories from Pulp Fiction's Golden Age

AND it *was* a golden age.

The 1930s and 1940s were a vibrant, seminal time for a gigantic audience of eager readers, probably the largest per capita audience of readers in American history. The magazine racks were chock-full of publications with ragged trims, garish cover art, cheap brown pulp paper, low cover prices—and the most excitement you could hold in your hands.

"Pulp" magazines, named for their rough-cut, pulpwood paper, were a vehicle for more amazing tales than Scheherazade could have told in a million and one nights. Set apart from higher-class "slick" magazines, printed on fancy glossy paper with quality artwork and superior production values, the pulps were for the "rest of us," adventure story after adventure story for people who liked to *read*. Pulp fiction authors were no-holds-barred entertainers—real storytellers. They were more interested in a thrilling plot twist, a horrific villain or a white-knuckle adventure than they were in lavish prose or convoluted metaphors.

The sheer volume of tales released during this wondrous golden age remains unmatched in any other period of literary history—hundreds of thousands of published stories in over nine hundred different magazines. Some titles lasted only an issue or two; many magazines succumbed to paper shortages during World War II, while others endured for decades yet. Pulp fiction remains as a treasure trove of stories you can read, stories you can love, stories you can remember. The stories were driven by plot and character, with grand heroes, terrible villains, beautiful damsels (often in distress), diabolical plots, amazing places, breathless romances. The readers wanted to be taken beyond the mundane, to live adventures far removed from their ordinary lives—and the pulps rarely failed to deliver.

In that regard, pulp fiction stands in the tradition of all memorable literature. For as history has shown, good stories are much more than fancy prose. William Shakespeare, Charles Dickens, Jules Verne, Alexandre Dumas—many of the greatest literary figures wrote their fiction for the readers, not simply literary colleagues and academic admirers. And writers for pulp magazines were no exception. These publications reached an audience that dwarfed the circulations of today's short story magazines. Issues of the pulps were scooped up and read by over thirty million avid readers each month.

Because pulp fiction writers were often paid no more than a cent a word, they had to become prolific or starve. They also had to write aggressively. As Richard Kyle, publisher and editor of *Argosy*, the first and most long-lived of the pulps, so pointedly explained: "The pulp magazine writers, the best of them, worked for markets that did not write for critics or attempt to satisfy timid advertisers. Not having to answer to anyone other than their readers, they wrote about human beings on the edges of the unknown, in those new lands the future would explore. They wrote for what we would become, not for what we had already been."

Some of the more lasting names that graced the pulps include H. P. Lovecraft, Edgar Rice Burroughs, Robert E. Howard, Max Brand, Louis L'Amour, Elmore Leonard, Dashiell Hammett, Raymond Chandler, Erle Stanley Gardner, John D. MacDonald, Ray Bradbury, Isaac Asimov, Robert Heinlein—and, of course, L. Ron Hubbard.

In a word, he was among the most prolific and popular writers of the era. He was also the most enduring—hence this series—and certainly among the most legendary. It all began only months after he first tried his hand at fiction, with L. Ron Hubbard tales appearing in *Thrilling Adventures, Argosy, Five-Novels Monthly, Detective Fiction Weekly, Top-Notch, Texas Ranger, War Birds, Western Stories,* even *Romantic Range.* He could write on any subject, in any genre, from jungle explorers to deep-sea divers, from G-men and gangsters, cowboys and flying aces to mountain climbers, hard-boiled detectives and spies. But he really began to shine when he turned his talent to science fiction and fantasy of which he authored nearly fifty novels or novelettes to forever change the shape of those genres.

Following in the tradition of such famed authors as Herman Melville, Mark Twain, Jack London and Ernest Hemingway, Ron Hubbard actually lived adventures that his own characters would have admired—as an ethnologist among primitive tribes, as prospector and engineer in hostile climes, as a captain of vessels on four oceans. He even wrote a series of articles for *Argosy*, called "Hell Job," in which he lived and told of the most dangerous professions a man could put his hand to.

Finally, and just for good measure, he was also an accomplished photographer, artist, filmmaker, musician and educator. But he was first and foremost a *writer*, and that's the L. Ron Hubbard we come to know through the pages of this volume.

This library of Stories from the Golden Age presents the best of L. Ron Hubbard's fiction from the heyday of storytelling, the Golden Age of the pulp magazines. In these eighty volumes, readers are treated to a full banquet of 153 stories, a kaleidoscope of tales representing every imaginable genre: science fiction, fantasy, western, mystery, thriller, horror, even romance—action of all kinds and in all places.

Because the pulps themselves were printed on such inexpensive paper with high acid content, issues were not meant to endure. As the years go by, the original issues of every pulp from *Argosy* through *Zeppelin Stories* continue crumbling into brittle, brown dust. This library preserves the L. Ron Hubbard tales from that era, presented with a distinctive look that brings back the nostalgic flavor of those times.

L. Ron Hubbard's Stories from the Golden Age has something for every taste, every reader. These tales will return you to a time when fiction was good clean entertainment and the most fun a kid could have on a rainy afternoon or the best thing an adult could enjoy after a long day at work.

Pick up a volume, and remember what reading is supposed to be all about. Remember curling up with a *great story.*

—Kevin J. Anderson

KEVIN J. ANDERSON *is the author of more than ninety critically acclaimed works of speculative fiction, including The Saga of Seven Suns, the continuation of the Dune Chronicles with Brian Herbert, and his* New York Times *bestselling novelization of L. Ron Hubbard's* Ai! Pedrito!

Mister Tidwell, Gunner

Mister Tidwell, Gunner

MISTER TIDWELL looked very calm standing there against the rail of the *Swiftsure*, but his outward appearance was no indication of the volcanic fires of loathing which seethed behind his small eyeglasses and bubbled beneath his gray frock coat.

Had anyone on the *Swiftsure* been told about those fires, he would have laughed heartily and long in the honest fashion of a Royal Navy tar.

The nub of Mister Tidwell's grievance was this. Here in the midst of rolling drums and clamorous trumpets which called to quarters, his purpose was lost. In a moment, if he did not like a taste of the cat, he would have to go below, far below into the evil smelling cockpit where the surgeon and his assistants were even now preparing for the toll.

The French man-o'-war had grown into a white sail mountain out of the Mediterranean blue, a bone in her teeth, looking like a mad dog frothing at the mouth, abristle with seventy-four naval cannon.

This, the high tide of the Napoleonic Wars, was the year 1798. Horatio Nelson, that quaint, efficient little man, was back on the sea, his right sleeve empty, his cheeks sunken with the effects of nine months of suffering in England.

The hot summer days were filled with ugly misgivings.

England, her Continental Alliance split apart, was suffering a dark day. And Nelson, the poor devil, was about to become the butt of a political fiasco solely because Boney's fleet had left Toulon for parts unknown and because Nelson, dismasted in a gale, had been unable to track the French across the trackless sea.

The whole, vibrant problem amounted to one question. Where were the French?

Alexandria? No, Nelson had called in. Asia Minor? No! Syracuse? No!

And here, rising like a ghost out of the seas came a French man-o'-war ready to do battle, nay, anxious to fight. The whereabouts of Boney's fleet must be muted at all costs. The French must take India. They must drive England out of the Mediterranean.

And the *Swiftsure*, all alone in the lazy blue expanse, girded the loins of her fighting men and prepared to deal iron in grape and canister doses.

And Mister Tidwell, pushed back and forth by hurrying gun crews and anxious Marines, gazed somberly at the approaching vessel and murmured a wish that he might be able to witness just one engagement in the light and air.

Two midshipmen, gold lace stiff and militant, scrambled up on the bulwark, small swords clanking, and began their ascent into the shrouds.

Mister Tidwell watched them go. Harvey and Sloan. Twelve years old, future officers, two of an uncontrollable band of twenty-four who harassed officers and men and Mister Tidwell without mercy.

Especially Mister Tidwell. He was their schoolmaster.

The crack brained idea which sent young men of twelve to sea, fostered in the dim past by King Charles, who thought his navy needed officers trained from infancy, had only been capped by another king's thought that these urchins should have the benefits of schooling at the hands of a trained master.

Mister Tidwell, along with several score of well-meaning professors, had long suffered the effects of those laws.

The small pay and the arduous life offered little attraction to any man of the day, much less a learned gentleman, and so His Majesty had been forced to conceive a stratagem which was nothing more than literary press ganging.

Two years before Mister Tidwell had written a paper. A mild, well worded paper, which dealt with the tax system. For that he had been sent to sea. And here he was, standing in the *Swiftsure's* scuppers, watching battle approach, knowing that he was even now late for the cockpit.

Marines swarmed up the ratlines, white crossbelts shimmering, muskets clenched, faces strained as they took their posts in the crosstrees. Mister Tidwell envied those Marines. Their sole duty consisted of taking pot shots at Marines in the rigging of the French ships, and what if they did die? They at least stayed out in the sun and air.

The long and short of Mister Tidwell's aversion to answering that call to quarters was blood.

A horizontal plume of smoke rapped out from the Frenchman's bow chasers. Round shot smashed solidly into the rail. Splinters sang like shrapnel. Two sailors clutched their lacerated faces and leaned sickly against their guns. One

5

of them looked at the maw of the hatch from whence came a stream of powder monkeys bearing their leathern buckets. He looked away again and strove to staunch the flow of blood with his white cotton shirt. No, that gunner certainly did not want to go below to the hospital.

The Frenchman was a quarter of a mile away, swinging into position for a broadside. On the *Swiftsure,* drums still rolled and trumpets blared, filling Mister Tidwell with uneasiness.

Gun captains blew on their matches. A twenty-four pounder spurted flame from muzzle and touchhole, leaped up and slammed back on the deck, splintering a wooden wheel. The shot sang through the Frenchman's rigging.

The broadside smashed out, enveloping the entire enemy ship with smoke. Sails and spars rained on the *Swiftsure*'s deck. A Marine came down like a shot tropical bird, hitting the planks solidly to roll over on his face. An officer leaned over him for a moment, hand pressed against the crimsoning crossbelts, and then jerked his thumb toward the rail. The Marine was thrown over the side.

Lucky, thought Mister Tidwell. The man hadn't lived to see the cockpit in action.

A hand fell on Tidwell's shoulder. A petty officer, face contorted with excitement and anger, shook the gray coat and sent Mister Tidwell hurtling toward the hatch.

A midshipman, holding a musket bigger than he was, paused in his ascent up a ratline long enough to grin. Mister Tidwell reproved the boy with a glance and then went below.

No one paid any attention to him on the second gun deck. The cannon had begun to fire, bucking out of line, filling the place with choking fumes. Mister Tidwell paused for a moment, reluctant to go below again. He saw the sweating torsos of the gunners through the dim welter of round shot, flying splinters, gashed beams and exploding guns.

He sighed, and then shrugging his small shoulders inside his gray frock coat, he adjusted his eye glasses and went down another ladder to the third gun deck.

The stream of black powder monkeys and their black cargoes choked the passageway for a moment. Mister Tidwell stood aside to let them by. Powder was strewn all over the planking. One match would finish the ship. It was ever thus.

Mister Tidwell went aft, ducking his head to avoid the beams. A tall man was forced to take to his hands and knees through this passageway. The cockpit was ahead.

A great lantern filled with sputtering candles burned against the beams. The midshipmen slept here when things were peaceful. Now the midshipmen's chests had been drawn together to make a low table. A piece of tarpaulin, already black with blood, was spread over the surface.

The surgeon, a tall, gaunt impassive gentleman, stood over a small stove heating his saws and knives and soldering irons. His assistants were placing buckets all about the improvised table, making ready for the men soon to come.

This was Mister Tidwell's battle station. Here he was no longer schoolmaster to the midshipmen, he was part of the surgeon's machine.

"About time," muttered an assistant. "Peel off that coat. Hear those guns? They'll be coming down here soon."

Mister Tidwell peeled off the gray coat, folded it up and

placed it in the corner. He felt nauseated already. The smell of the bilge, mixed with powder smoke, stale food, dirty clothes and dried blood was already affecting him.

The cannons barked overhead. Their wheels roared across the upper decks in constant discord. The *Swiftsure* lurched and rolled under the impacts of recoil and canister, by courtesy of the French.

Mister Tidwell felt some interest in the guns. He had devoted considerable time and much mathematics to the study of ordnance. He felt no interest at all in surgery. But he rolled up his sleeves, squinted his eyes through the bad light and waited nervously for things to happen.

The first victim was a brawny lad, carried between two sailors. The man's eyes were narrow with pain and his mouth was set. His leg was mangled at the thigh. He lived only through grace of a tight tourniquet.

Mister Tidwell knew his duty. He picked up a bottle of rum and shoved the mouth between the brawny lad's teeth. He let the fluid gurgle until the surgeon, in an impassive voice, said, "That's enough. We'll need some for the others."

Thereupon, Mister Tidwell and three assistants seized the man, threw him upon the low table and the surgeon went to work. Mister Tidwell placed a wooden peg in the victim's mouth so that he would not break his teeth.

The surgeon, with a heated knife, slashed the flesh away from the bone in one swift, semi-circular slash. He snatched up the saw and went through the living bone.

The mangled limb was thrown into a bucket, the stump was swiftly wrapped, the brawny lad, eyes wild with agony, ceased to struggle in the grip of the assistants. He was thrown to one side.

Mister Tidwell looked behind him. The men were piling up like cord wood against the bulkhead. Rifle wounds, splinters, charred faces from flarebacks, smashed hands, crushed arms . . . Mister Tidwell swallowed hard and selected the next victim.

This was a bullet hole in the chest. The surgeon waived aside the rum. This was not a serious operation. A soldering iron was taken from the stove. Mister Tidwell and the assistants had to hold hard to keep the victim still. The iron was plunged deep in the wound.

With a tremor, the sailor laid very still. Blood was frothing out of his mouth.

"He's dead," said the surgeon, and motioned for the man to be cast aside.

The work went on. The buckets were growing full. Blood dripped slowly to the floor and ran in rivulets toward the bulkheads.

Mister Tidwell administered rum until his arms were tired and when the rum gave out he gave them gin. And when the gin gave out, he gave them nothing. They bore their agony in silence as well as they could.

A strapping big Marine was carried in and laid with the others on the floor. His brown eyes were big and staring as he watched the surgeon work. The slash of the knife through living flesh seemed to fascinate him. The Marine's whole arm was crushed.

Mister Tidwell turned just in time to see the Marine

crawling away. He tried to screen the escape but the surgeon said, "Bring him next."

They threw the Marine on the table. They ripped off his crossbelts. They tore his scarlet coat. He turned his face away, looking at the big lantern. The grate of the saw could be heard above the rumble of cannon wheels. Quietly, the Marine fainted.

Hours and hours it went on. The cockpit filled with men who had received the administrations of the surgeon. Then at last the cannonading stopped and the ship became quiet.

Mister Tidwell, splattered with blood, wanted to go on deck, but there was still work to be done. He was given a sponge and told to bathe out the lesser wounds. One sponge to a dozen men.

Mister Tidwell, working beside these men who were making the sea safe for British merchant ships, men who had been dragged forcefully away by the press gangs, knew the futility of his work. Once he had written a paper on medicine and infection. He had some inkling of germs and the reasons for the spread of gangrene. He knew that half these men would die in a week, another quarter in a month and that the rest would hobble through life with wrecked health.

But he worked on with his sponge, under orders, his frail shoulders bent, his eyes very tired, his bony hands shaking.

How different this was from the quiet thoughtfulness of Oxford where he had spent the greater part of his life. Had anyone told him three years before that in the summer of 1798 he would be in the Mediterranean administering to wounded men under the direction of a coldblooded surgeon, he would have thought it an immense joke.

He could bear his duties of teaching midshipmen, however arrogant, however unruly they might be, but each time an engagement came close, he shivered at the thought of the cockpit.

It was night before he got on deck. The battle had been a draw, but the *Swiftsure* had been unable to pursue the Frenchman. However, the losses were not without compensation. The French vessel had headed for Alexandria.

Mister Tidwell listened to his midshipmen. One of them was dead, another bore a glorious bandage about his brow where a langrage shot had grazed him.

Harvey, who had acquitted himself with honor by pistoling a French seaman, drew himself up proudly and walked along the stained deck with not a little swagger, excusable in a boy twelve years of age and a future admiral.

"I should think," said Mister Tidwell, "that the French would be in Alexandria if the vessel headed that way."

Harvey's voice was shrill and full of scorn. "What the hell would you know about it, hiding down in the cockpit all during the fight? We cleaned up Boney's scow and no mistake. She had to head in for repairs, that's what. She damned well needs them too."

"But by my casual observance of naval tactics, reporting to the commander would seem to be more vital than refitting a single ship."

Sloan looked about at his brother midshipmen and laughed.

11

Mister Tidwell leaned against the bulkhead and turned his back on them. They had been invested with too much authority, they were undisciplined, brawling and intolerant.

Harvey forgot about Mister Tidwell. He started a story about how he had helped capture a loose cannon in the 'tween decks, how it had mangled three gunners before it had at last become roped.

Mister Tidwell leaned far over the rail, very ill. He had attended to those gunners.

Three days later, the *Swiftsure* contacted the *Vanguard* on the high seas and drew in close to report her engagement with the enemy.

Nelson was on the quarterdeck, sleeve empty, face pale, eyes deep and troubled with his problems but, at the same time aflame with the will to destroy the French for once and for all.

Mister Tidwell timidly filched the watch officers glass and studied Nelson with it. There, thought Mister Tidwell, was a great man, a humane man. It was not because of Nelson that Mister Tidwell served in the cockpit during battles.

Mister Tidwell saw something further. Nelson was about his size, about the same build. Even this remote connection made Mister Tidwell feel better. Everything would be all right. Nelson would see to that.

The news came back from the *Vanguard* with the *Swiftsure's* boat. Sloan, who had coxswained the jolly boat, brought his brother midshipmen—and Mister Tidwell—the news.

"He's smart," said Sloan, with all the authority of a flag

captain. "He says the damned French frog eaters are at Alexandria. He says we're going down there, too, and knock the hell out of them."

"I thought they'd be there," ventured Mister Tidwell.

"You thought!" said Sloan very scornful. "All you know is your damned arithmetic."

Mister Tidwell removed his German spectacles, polished them with the tail of his gray coat, and said, "Someday, Mister Sloan, someone is going to spank you very thoroughly."

Sloan's face turned scarlet. His breath hissed between his clenched teeth. He drew himself up like a fighting cock and said, "Perhaps, Mister Tidwell, you don't know who the hell you're talking to. In the future, allow me to remind you that a further display of insubordination will require me to have you flogged for discourtesy to a midshipman."

It all sounded very ridiculous, but Mister Tidwell held his tongue and contented himself by merely turning away. The terrible, heart breaking part of it was that Sloan was utterly correct. As a future officer and as a present midshipman, Sloan's authority was monstrous, as was that of the other twenty-two.

"So," said Mister Tidwell to himself, tucking his hands under the tail of his coat and slapping knuckles against palm, "So I don't know anything but arithmetic. And it often seems that I do not even know that."

He saw that they were getting under weigh, heading into formation behind the rest of the "liners." A terrible sense of futility came over him. He felt so all alone, so keenly that he did not belong. He was a civilian among sailors and Marines and officers.

And he knew that another battle would mean another siege in the cockpit.

The injustice of the thing rankled in his small breast. He knew all the theory of ordnance, of sail, of military tactics. Hadn't he studied them? He knew mathematics beyond the scope of any officer in the fleet. Hadn't he written several papers on them? He was the size of Nelson.

And yet in battle he had to endure the horrors of a slaughterhouse just because he had once written a paper which criticised the tax system—had criticised it mildly, but well.

What wouldn't he give for his small desk at Oxford now?

All that night the *Swiftsure* sailed with the fleet, and news came filtering through to Mister Tidwell that the campaign was going very badly indeed. The fact worried him on Nelson's account. Too bad poor Nelson had come back from England to find things going so wrong.

It seemed that Boney had taken everything and anything. Malta had fallen to the tricolor and England was aghast, convinced that Nelson's wound had ruined him, that the cause was lost against France. England, in common with Nelson's men, saw the whole world turning red and white and blue before their very eyes.

But not until the morrow did they know just how badly things had gone. When they came into the area of the Nile, they saw the French flag whipping in a desert wind. Nelson and Mister Tidwell sighed. Then Egypt had fallen to France.

14

The big fleet at Toulon which had escaped during Nelson's absence had effected a landing, had taken the country.

Nelson, thought Mister Tidwell, was through. He felt very badly about it. Nelson could not have helped losing the fleet and Boney that way. Nelson could hardly have stopped Boney from landing in Egypt.

And then, sailing through the yellow water, blinded by the light-haze of the afternoon sun, they caught sight of de Brueys' fleet lying at anchor in Aboukir Bay.

Nelson's captains groaned. De Brueys was astute, assured, almost impudent in the disposition of his forces. Aboukir Bay is about fifteen miles wide, almost a sea in itself, but the western side was silted up, making navigation impossible.

De Brueys, having escorted Napoleon's army to Egypt, had chosen the spot because of its natural protection. He had swung his line of ships in close to the shore, stringing them out and anchoring them so that they presented nothing less than a line of formidable fortresses. De Brueys knew that he would have to be attacked from the seaward side and he had already prepared his seaward batteries and had planted other batteries ashore to protect his position.

The French fleet consisted of the mammoth *L'Orient*, the greatest ship of her time and the flagship, nine seventy-fours, three eighties and four imposing frigates.

Gun for gun, Nelson could hold his own. But to assail such a group of floating fortresses seemed a foolhardy move. The French seemingly thumbed their noses and rode quietly at anchor.

The flagship of the French, the hundred and twenty gun

Orient was at the head of line, facing north. Behind her the others strung themselves out, glinting in the sunlight, watchful and ready.

"Oh, my," said Mister Tidwell to himself, "the poor chap is finished now." And he leaned disconsolately upon the rail, looking at the bare yards of the French.

In a way, Mister Tidwell was very glad. No cockpit this time. But even so, it seemed a shame that they would be unable to sever Napoleon's communication lines by destroying his fleet. The fleet looked so inviting. If the French lost their fleet, thought Mister Tidwell, Napoleon in Egypt would be like an ant in a bowl of pea soup. No supplies, no communication.

He became so engrossed in the tactical problem which presented itself that he wandered up to the quarterdeck. The officers there were far too excited to pay him any heed and he managed to borrow the glass again.

Looking toward the *Vanguard* which made slow way under shortened sail, Mister Tidwell saw a black coated figure on the deck. The empty sleeve marked Nelson. Poor chap, thought Mister Tidwell. Nelson was pacing up and down, up and down, stopping every few moments like a caged animal trying to figure a way through the bars.

Then Mister Tidwell inspected the *Orient*. An enormous vessel. Hundred and twenty guns they said. He tried to count the open ports and failed because of their number. He fancied a bluff, frock coated gentleman on the *Orient*'s quarterdeck to be de Brueys.

Gigs were putting out from the drifting English fleet, taking the captains to the *Vanguard* for their orders. Never in his life had Nelson gone into an engagement without explaining everything to his "band of captains." Mister Tidwell watched enviously.

Soon the captains came back and Sloan came out of the gig very important, immediately seeking his fellows. Mister Tidwell moved close to the midshipman to hear what the orders were.

"He's smart," said Sloan. "Damned smart. He says 'where the French can swing, the English can anchor.' We're going in there and beat them at their own game. The wind is from the north. We drift down upon them and drop our hooks, then pay out cable until we get right alongside and give them hell for glory. S'help me, it's going to be a fine fight!"

It was a long shot, thought Mister Tidwell, but Nelson could do it. Nelson could do anything. That decided, Mister Tidwell thought about himself and remembered with a cringing stomach that he would have another session in the cockpit.

Anything but that!

His eyes, peering through his glasses, took on a rebellious look. His small, well shaven jaw set stubbornly. He put his hands under the tail of his gray coat, smacked knuckles against palm and muttered, "Anything but that!"

But if he failed to report to quarters, he'd get sixty lashes with the cat—and sixty lashes to a man of Mister Tidwell's small stature was as good as death.

Drums began to roll throughout the fleet. Trumpets blared. Mister Tidwell thrilled to the martial music and then remembered the cockpit. He sidled toward the hatch, driving

17

himself on, thinking about dying men, buckets, severed limbs, running blood, the flesh and red-heated saws through grating bone.

Marines were running for the rigging. Gun crews were ripping off their shirts. Powder monkeys began to scamper. The midshipmen, bawling orders in piping voices, ran to their posts.

Mister Tidwell looked at the men, suddenly assailed by a horrible sensation. These strong, rough sailors were here now, whole in body. In a matter of a few hours, many of them would be below, held down by the assistant surgeons, while they were maimed for life.

Rebellion against such a thing welled up in Mister Tidwell's narrow chest. Nervously he avoided looking at the men.

Part of the British fleet was putting in on the seaward side. The remainder were headed for a desperate chance. They were going to drop their hooks between the French and the shore.

Mister Tidwell appreciated Nelson's deduction. Nothing in the way of double anchors had been dropped from the French vessels. Therefore the Frenchmen were perfectly free to swing. Nelson's phrase, "Where there is room for a Frenchman to swing, there is room for a Briton to anchor," looked very pale. Only an expert seaman could warp a big "liner" in between the French and the shore.

The sun was going down, painting the world an ominous blood red. The *Goliath* in the hands of Captain Foley, headed in toward the *Guerrier*. The *Swiftsure* was behind the other ships, holding off until the last moment.

Mister Tidwell still lingered on deck, fascinated by the gory sky and the approaching battle. He caught his breath when Foley swept in alongside the Frenchman, broke through the line and swung in by the shore. As he passed, Foley loosed a thundering broadside. The *Goliath* and the *Guerrier* reeled away from each other, swallowed in smoke and flame. Foley went on and dropped his anchor on the port quarter of the *Conquerant*. An audacious move, dropping that anchor as though there to stay.

Mister Tidwell had no more seen the anchor drop than Captain Hood and his *Zealous* swung in and anchored on the port bow of the *Guerrier*. The four ships were immediately engulfed in their own powder smoke, fighting an arm's length away from each other, hammering wicked bursts of canister and grape into wooden hulls, smashing down men and rigging, disrupting guns, sending the water up in mammoth geysers.

Darkness came a moment later. All that marked the ships was the flashing of cannon. Mister Tidwell could barely make out the *Audacious*, the *Theseus* and the *Orion* as they smashed their ways through the French line and took up their positions between the vessels and the shoals.

The *Vanguard*, bearing Nelson, slid in from the seaward side and dropped anchor almost touching the *Spartiate*. Both ships immediately began a savage cannonade at close range. The rest of the British swung in from the seaward side.

It was fully dark now. The water was painted scarlet by the blaze of powder. The din was so enormous that when the *Swiftsure*'s cannon began to go, Mister Tidwell did not even hear them.

19

And still Mister Tidwell did not go below into the cockpit.

The British *Bellerophon,* just ahead of the *Swiftsure,* sailed quickly in upon the mighty *Orient,* de Brueys' flagship. The *Orient* loosed a thunderous broadside, lighting up every wooden pin in the British vessel.

The *Bellerophon,* decks raked, sails in ribbons, reeled on in toward the shore to engage the rest of the French fleet.

The *Swiftsure* was running side by side with the *Alexander.* By common consent, the two attacked the great *Orient,* one on either side like terriers pulling down a wolf.

Men began to fall on the *Swiftsure's* deck. The plunging cannon slammed back and forth, alternately touched off and dragged inboard for reloading. The gun captains, great shadows against the red flare, worked feverishly at their charges.

Mister Tidwell had completely forgotten himself. He hugged the rail, oblivious of flying splinters and screaming grape, until a rough hand whirled him about. He was staring into the powder-blackened face of a young lieutenant.

"Get below!" howled the officer. "I'm reporting you. You'll pay for this! Get below!"

Mister Tidwell deflated. He'd be reported. Who would have seen him in all this excitement?

A ball ripped past his face and smashed into the mast. A gunner, shoulders smashed into a red mess, reeled against Mister Tidwell and slid to the deck. The thought of the cockpit made Mister Tidwell writhe.

Close at hand he saw the ratlines. The lieutenant was gone. Mister Tidwell, jaw set, gray coat flapping about his legs, reached up and pulled himself off the deck.

He climbed swiftly, terror tugging at him as he thought of the surgeon's knife.

The *Swiftsure* was in under the *Orient*'s rail, overshadowed by the heaving bulk. As Mister Tidwell climbed he could see the battle stretching out on toward the shore. The night was scarlet, tumultuous.

A rifle ball tugged his sleeve, but he did not mind it. He'd get flogged in the morning, but right now he was free.

He saw a flash of white above him. A Marine was in the crosstrees with his musket, sniping at the *Orient*'s quarterdeck.

The Marine, his smoke-blackened face in startling contrast to his teeth, looked amazed at the ship's schoolmaster. "Get down! Damme, you'll get killed!"

Mister Tidwell calmly pulled himself up to the yard and perched there, high over the pitching deck, like a bird on a flagpole. "Go ahead," said Mister Tidwell. "Pray don't let me bother you."

The Marine had other things to worry about. His shiny black hat with its cockade was gone. His crossbelts were awry. "That ——— —— —— in the mizzen," he rattled. "He's tryin' to get the bloomin' hofficers!" The musket exploded and Mister Tidwell watched the *Orient*'s mizzen for the other sniper.

"Missed the ——," said the Marine, expectorating out of the corner of his mouth and reloading in the wind.

Abruptly the man sat upright. Mister Tidwell saw a third eye appear in his forehead. Mister Tidwell knew the man was already dead. The Marine swayed stiffly back, slowly, slowly, until he toppled off the yard and plummeted down.

Mister Tidwell almost lost his balance in retrieving the musket, the powder and the balls. He scowled thoughtfully at the musket. He had never before handled one, but he had read a great deal.

He poured the powder down the muzzle, rammed in the wadding, dropped the bullet in, rammed it down and then with an eager light in his pale eyes, surveyed the mizzen of the *Orient*.

A flash appeared there, close beside the mast. On the *Swiftsure*'s deck, an officer dropped leadenly. Mister Tidwell looked to the rudimentary sights of the gun.

"Two hundred and twenty feet," muttered Mister Tidwell. He aimed and pulled the trigger. Nothing happened. Embarrassed at his oversight, he filled the priming pan and closed it. This gave him further pause.

"Flintlock using pyrites," muttered Mister Tidwell. "British Army. Effective range set at one hundred yards. Battle sights one hundred yards. If I set this at . . ."

When he fired again, he aimed exactly one foot above the French sniper's head. The man fell forward, swiftly, disappearing into the cluttered mêlée on deck.

"There," said Mister Tidwell, and reloaded again.

He saw a man with gold lace rushing along the line of guns on the *Orient*'s deck. He frowned thoughtfully again. "If I fire at his feet, the downward trajectory will be compensated."

Accordingly he fired at the officer's feet. The Frenchman doubled up like a jackknife and pitched into the scuppers.

"And there," said Mister Tidwell.

*When he fired again, he aimed exactly one foot above the
French sniper's head. The man fell forward, swiftly,
disappearing into the cluttered mêlée on deck.*

A moment later he was aware that his presence had become known. Splinters flew out of the mast beside his head. He did not duck. He reasoned that it was useless to duck after you heard the bullet strike. He calmly reloaded his musket and watched for another flash in the Frenchman's shrouds. It came presently. Mister Tidwell saw that his man was almost naked, clinging to a yard with the agility of an ape.

Mister Tidwell aimed a foot and a half above the man's white face. The sniper fell two feet and then brought up short to sway entangled in the lines.

"That will teach you, my good fellow," said Mister Tidwell. He wiped off his glasses and surveyed the battle which had spread out fanwise behind the *Orient*. He could see the *Alexander* through the Frenchman's rigging, hammering into the huge bulk with hot, flaming cannon.

Mister Tidwell felt guilty for a moment. He had deserted his post and a flogging would await him in the morning, but, and thank God for that, he did not have to stand the cockpit this night.

Something moved just under him and he looked down, full into the face of Sloan. Sloan was trying to unfurl a sail with the help of two seamen. His midshipman's jacket was rumpled, his white face looked scared.

"Damme!" cried Sloan. "What the hell are you doing up there?"

Mister Tidwell started down. Sloan, too amazed to do more than stare, hung on and watched him come.

Silently, Mister Tidwell walked the yard, unlashed the

canvas there and came back. The sail dropped out and barked in the wind. "Sloan," said Mister Tidwell, "if you say anything about this, I'm certain that you will live to regret it and no longer."

Sloan gaped. He backed away toward the ratlines. Mister Tidwell made a move toward him and Sloan scampered down. Mister Tidwell chuckled to himself.

The *Swiftsure* had drawn off from the *Orient* but returned with a sudden rush like that of a cornered rat who suddenly decides to risk destruction if only to wreak vengeance upon an enemy.

Mister Tidwell started back up to the crosstrees a few feet over his head. The mast was trembling. It shook harder like a tree under the felling ax of a woodsman.

Cannon fire had weakened it. Now it was about to fall.

The *Swiftsure*'s tempestuous rush brought up with a crash against the bulwarks of the *Orient*. It happened in a fraction of a second. Mister Tidwell was unable to hold on.

The mast snapped off under the impact. Mister Tidwell felt himself catapulted out into space. His only thought was a hope that he would be killed outright instead of in the cockpit.

Blackness engulfed him. A line whipped past his face. Wood smashed him across the middle, knocking the breath out of him. Half unconscious, he held staunchly to canvas and yard, fighting to get back his breath, surprised that he was still alive.

A minute or two later he found strength enough to look about him. A long drop still lay between himself and the deck. He inched his way in toward the mast, wondering that it was still firm, thinking that he must have been mistaken in thinking it snapped off.

Mister Tidwell then became aware that he was not alone on the yard. The fellow who slowly approached him was not a member of the *Swiftsure*'s crew. His uniform was wrong.

A Frenchman!

And what was a Frenchman doing on a English ship? Something was wrong. Mister Tidwell's eyes focused, though none too well since he had lost his glasses, on a sailor's knife in the other's hand.

Mister Tidwell considered the situation. Something hard and heavy pressed against his side. The bag of bullets. He took them out, hefting them. They made a wonderful bludgeon.

Then he started in, meeting the Frenchman halfway. The bullets swung down. The knife came up. The Frenchman grabbed Mister Tidwell's shoulders. Avoiding the knife, Mister Tidwell came down a second time with the bullets.

Oddly, the grip on his collar loosened. The Frenchman swooped away from him, growing smaller and smaller, falling through the lighted space of firing guns. Then the fellow disappeared.

Mister Tidwell reached for his glasses to wipe them, discovered that they were gone and proceeded on down the yard toward the crosstrees. When he looked around him, he knew he was in the rigging of the *Orient*. The *Swiftsure* was already drawing off, leaving the rubbish of its main lying across the *Orient*'s deck.

Mister Tidwell reached out, exploring the small platform for a weapon. Something burned him and he almost went off his giddy perch with surprise. On closer examination he found a burning match which had touched his fingers. Hanging from a peg he discovered a canvas bag which seemed to contain large coconuts.

He drew one out and inspected it. It was black with a corrugated surface and from its snout there dangled a length of fuse.

"A grenade," said Mister Tidwell thoughtfully. Then this was what the Frenchman had been doing in the rigging. Mister Tidwell grew a little angry. The fellow had been throwing the things down on the deck of the *Swiftsure*.

"We'll see how the Frenchman likes it," muttered Mister Tidwell, looking down at the swarming expanse of the *Orient*. He held the grenade gingerly in his right hand, the match in his left.

One gun down there seemed to be firing more steadily than the others. It was, decided Mister Tidwell, a bomb thrower. Certainly such a thing should be stopped.

He measured the distance down with his eye. "If I toss this away from me as though the target were only ten feet distant, the trajectory will be perfect."

He lighted the fuse, allowed it to get going and then made the toss. An instant later the bomb thrower was devoured in smoke. When the smoke cleared, by the light of action lanterns, Mister Tidwell could see nothing of the crew.

"Hmm," said Mister Tidwell. "Very effective."

27

He took another grenade and studied the deck. It seemed to him that the battle was still in favor of the French. Evidently something was holding up the attack. It worried him.

He saw a group of officers on the quarterdeck which could be reached by tossing a bomb over the mizzen yard. The officers were pointing at the *Swiftsure*, directing the fire.

"Ah," said Mister Tidwell, igniting the grenade, "I'm afraid I can't have that, my good fellows."

He tossed the bomb with a quick underhand motion. It soared over the mizzen yard and dropped down, gracefully. An instant later it rolled along the planking and exploded with a red sparked flash. Due to the fact that the action lantern there was blown out by the concussion, Mister Tidwell was unable to see the effects of the throw.

He looked down at the deck again. Men were running about, pointing up and yelling.

"Ah, they have discovered me," said Mister Tidwell, regretfully. An officer had stopped with drawn pistols. He fired and the balls went shrieking past Mister Tidwell's head.

Mister Tidwell dropped a grenade. Men ran away from it and it rolled under a gun carriage, exploding there. The gun jumped grotesquely up and fell back smoldering.

Sailors started up the ratlines, cutlasses in hand. "It's all over, I'm afraid," said Mister Tidwell.

He studied the battle again. It became clear to him that the *Orient* was in the way. The *Orient*, at the apex of the French line, was the backbone of the defense. Nelson's strategy was rendered nothing by the position of the flagship.

Mister Tidwell thought about Nelson. "Poor little fellow,"

he murmured. Now Pitt would be able to do nothing for England with a new coalition on the continent. Napoleon would retain his transports and his communication, India would fall and Great Britain would no longer rule the seas. It was depressing, thought Mister Tidwell.

He looked at the sailors swarming up at him. He held a grenade in his palm, but it was no weapon against climbing men. He was thinking about Nelson and that empty sleeve.

Below him yawned the midships hatch. Straight down he could see flashes on the second gun deck. The deck, in the light of the action lanterns was dark about the ladder.

"Powder," said Mister Tidwell, thankfully. "Ah, yes, powder."

The leathern buckets, swiftly carried, always spilled their contents one way or another and the powder monkeys in the heat of the fray, were not too careful. That meant that a line of powder was strung from the hatch to the magazine.

Mister Tidwell sighed. "Poor little fellow. If this ship was to be obliterated . . ."

He touched a match to the grenade. The sailors were almost to him, coming swiftly. Mister Tidwell watched the fuse burn. There could be no miss this time. The powder magazine was directly under his mast. He had no illusions as to what would happen.

For a moment he listened to the incessant drumming of the guns. Then he loosed the black ball. It grew smaller and smaller. The explosion was a spreading fan of fire. Greenish tongues whipped along the planks in every direction. The powder was going.

Down the first ladder, down the second ladder, down the third ladder . . . Mister Tidwell held his breath.

Suddenly he felt as though he had been smashed by a monstrous fist. Flame shot across the world. Splinters and wreckage soared toward the scarlet sky.

Mister Tidwell, turning over and over through space, saw the vision of the cockpit and its buckets. He smiled softly to himself. One thing he wouldn't have to worry about. Not any more. Ever.

They picked him up at midnight, clinging hard to a bit of board, struggling in the strewn water. They were not bent on rescue work, those of the *Vanguard*. They were looking for the French admiral, de Brueys.

But they pulled Mister Tidwell out and laid him on the blood soaked planks to recuperate as best he could. Hard as his bed was, he slept as soon as he heard that the French fleet had surrendered after the explosion aboard the mammoth *Orient*.

The next morning he saw Nelson walking along the deck, preoccupied but complacent. The right sleeve was tucked into his tunic pocket. His hair was twisted into a long pigtail.

Mister Tidwell was sitting against the mast, striving to hide the scratches on his face for fear of the hospital. Nelson, seeing him, stopped short with surprise.

"Who is this man?" Nelson asked an officer.

Mister Tidwell stood up respectfully and bowed, answering the question himself. "I am Mister Tidwell, sir. Schoolmaster off the *Swiftsure*. I suppose they'll be looking for me, sir." He stopped, abashed at having said so much to so great a man.

"And why would they be looking for you?" said Nelson, affected by the tone of the man's voice.

"I suppose . . . for a flogging, sir."

"A flogging? Nonsense. Why should they flog a schoolmaster? I thought," he added with a humorous quirk on his mouth, "that the schoolmasters were supposed to do the flogging."

Mister Tidwell's eyes sought the deck. He felt very frail and tired and his thin shoulders bowed under the weight of his grief. Then he straightened up.

"I deserted my battle station, sir."

Nelson looked a little surprised. "And what is your battle station? How did you ever get off the *Swiftsure*?"

"I'm . . . I am supposed to help in the cockpit, sir, with the wounded you see. And I . . . I am completely unable to . . . to bear the . . . slaughterhouse, sir."

Nelson's eyes quickened. He stepped closer to Mister Tidwell. "Then you jumped over the side?"

"No sir. I mounted into the rigging, sir, and there took the place of a Marine who had been shot. I suppose I was a little sentimental, sir, but when they shot the Marine, I wanted to adjust matters. I suppose you had better restore me to the *Swiftsure*, sir. They'll be wanting to flog me, you understand."

"Wait. How did you leave the vessel?"

"The mast fell when the *Swiftsure* rammed the *Orient* and I was catapulted into the mainmast of the Frenchman."

31

"Extraordinary," said Nelson, genuinely interested. "Then what did you do?"

"I dropped a few grenades I found in the crosstrees, sir, just to defend myself you see. I realize I was acting without orders, that I had deserted my ship . . ."

"And the grenades exploded the powder magazine," finished Nelson. "And you knew that they would."

"I believe that is the way of it, sir. I was unduly sentimental, of course, but I was affected by the immovability of the *Orient* which obviously held up the attack. I thought it . . . quite a shame . . . that you, sir . . . "

Nelson was smiling, affectionately, indulgently. He stood back and looked at Mister Tidwell's short, slight body, at his rounded shoulders, at his bony hands, at the tatters of the gray coat.

"Mister Tidwell," said Nelson, "did you ever write a treatise on ordnance from Oxford?"

Startled, Mister Tidwell turned a dull red and started to draw back. But Nelson's arm was about his shoulder drawing him along toward the cabins aft.

"I have that treatise in my cabin," said Nelson, smiling. "A very informative piece of work, sir. A very informative piece of work. I had no idea of the history involved nor of the applicable mathematics."

Mister Tidwell immediately forgot that Nelson was Nelson. He saw the man as a man, and a wounded man at that, having a bandage about his head covering the gash cut by a langrage shot.

"Oh, yes," said Mister Tidwell. "The study of trajectory

is a very interesting matter. Newton's works on the subject seem to be constructed solely for the purposes of ordnance. Calculus plays its part, I assure you."

Nelson drew him into the cabin and looked into his shelf of books. He drew out a small brief which bore the name of Professor Tidwell, Oxford University, January 21, 1793.

Looking reverently at the pamphlet, Nelson shook his wounded head, an ironic twist to his mouth, and said, "So they had you in the cockpit, sawing off arms and legs. Professor, I can sympathize with you." He made a small, tired motion toward his empty sleeve and bandaged head. "I, too, know the cockpit.

"But then," said Nelson, "here I am, keeping you on your feet when you need a rest so badly. Pardon me. Make yourself comfortable, I'll send some clothes. And by the way, look into that mirror there and tell me who you see."

Mister Tidwell, much astonished, gazed at his haggard reflection. "Why . . . sir, Mister Tidwell, schoolmaster to the midshipmen of the HMS *Swiftsure*."

Nelson laughed and tapped the pamphlet on gunnery against his palm. "Yes? You think so, eh? Well, sir, let me assure you that that man you see in the mirror is none other than Captain Tidwell, gunnery officer to the British fleet in Mediterranean waters. On my honor be it."

And the great Nelson gave him a precise and respectful salute, there in the cabin of the *Vanguard*, off Alexandria, in sight of the still smoldering French fleet, on August the second, 1798.

Submarine

Submarine

SEVENTY-TWO hours before the submarine *SJ-9* took her last dive into the Pacific to rest a battered, capsized and entangled hulk on the ocean's murky floor, a motor sailer bumped gently against the dock at the end of San Diego's Broadway. The long open boat was filled to overflowing with a crowd of boisterous bluejackets, home from a Panama cruise. They jostled their way up the narrow gangway to the street, and after a few minutes of milling about, went their respective ways to ply their separate and collective vices.

The crowd thinned down until just one man stood in the arc-lit circle at the end of the wharf. He was a small man, but what he lacked in stature he made up in carriage and uniform. Everything about him was the height of regulation. That is, everything except his cap. In spite of the admiral's decree concerning white caps, this son of Neptune wore his stiffly starched headgear far on the back of his head, permitting a truant lock of hair to project itself into his worried eyes.

He glanced into all the shadows and then up the well-lighted thoroughfare, his brow puckering until he looked very fierce for so young a sailor. After standing still for several minutes, he lifted his jacket and sought with long fingers into the waistband of his pants. A somewhat crumpled letter came forth into the light.

Dearest Pinky,

I'm watching the papers every day for the fleet's return. It seems to me that all those admirals are being particularly mean not to let the *SJ-9* return ahead of time. Can't you do something about it? Well, I suppose not, but the second you set foot on the dock at—

A taxi lurched into the arc light with a scream of brakes. A very excited girl jumped out and ran the few steps to the sailor.

"Pinky!"

"Madge!"

Much to the sailor's surprise, he discovered that he had been kissing her for some time. The taximan was grinning. Pinky straightened his scarf and blushed.

"Well, how have you been?" He assumed an air of nonchalance.

"Oh, Pinky, I've just been sitting up there in that stuffy old room looking out at the bay for it seems years. I didn't think that old pigboat would ever bring you home."

"Shucks. When I start worrying about the *SJ-9* it'll be plenty of time for you to begin. Look what I brought you from Panama!" He stepped back into the shadow and came forth again carrying a small suitcase. He set it impressively before the girl and then stepped back much in the manner of a dog awaiting its master's approval.

Madge opened her large eyes even wider. "Pinky, you shouldn't 've."

"Well, open it up!"

She knelt beside the grip and presently dragged forth a varicolored Spanish shawl. "OOOH! It's wonderful!"

38

"Aw, it ain't anything. Just thought you'd like to have one, that's all."

She threw the shawl over her shoulder and kissed him again. The taximan was still grinning.

"C'mon, Madge. Let's go someplace. How about we take in Balboa?"

"All right, honey. The Japanese garden, remember?"

The taxi sped away up the wide avenue toward Balboa Park and a certain Japanese garden.

A sliver of a moon was trying to light up the reflecting pool, a million stars were prying into the shelter of ivy and wandering Jew. The gentle hum of traffic on a boulevard several hundred yards away added to the symphony of peace surrounding the two on the bench.

"Listen, honey. When do you go to sea again?"

"Oh, I forgot to tell you. Look here!" Pinky dragged out a liberty card on which was written *Seventy-two*. "That means the Navy will have to get along without me for three whole days!"

"I'm glad." Madge buried her brunette head in his shoulder. Her voice was muffled. "I wish you'd leave the Navy."

"Huh. What do you want me to do? Desert?"

"Even that."

"Listen, Madge. You know I only got eight months and a butt. That isn't long, is it?"

"For me it is." Madge looked up at his face. "You don't know how long it will be to me. You, you're different. At sea all the time, or lying alongside the *Farragut,* busy with your work. All I do is sit in that stuffy room and wish there had never been a Navy."

39

Pinky laughed. "If there hadn't been a Navy, how would you have met me?"

"Aw, Pinky, don't be like that. You don't know how terrible it is to sit still and think about you out there on the sea in that terrible pigboat!"

"Haven't I told you not to worry about the *SJ-9*? Say, honey, she's as safe as a battlewagon. There isn't a submarine in the fleet can beat her record. See here!" He presented her with an arm on which there glowed a white *E*. "For efficiency, that's what. Best gunnery. Best diving record. Greatest economy. That's what the *SJ-9* is like. Every doggoned sub in the fleet is bilious green with envy."

"But still, things happen, don't they? How about the *M-2*, the *S-4*, the—"

"Sure. But what can you expect fooling around with those old tubs? Built of salt and orange juice. No wonder they went down. No wonder. But the *SJ-9*, that's different!"

"Didn't you break a diving rudder in Panama?"

"Huh? Ah—sure we did. How did you know about it?"

"Aw gee, honey, every time I read about these things in the papers I feel awful. Listen, Pinky. Can't you get transferred to a destroyer or something that stays on top all the time? You got a chance, then."

"Say, haven't you heard about this type of diving lung we got? All you do is put the thing around your neck and walk out the hatch. Nothing to it. You couldn't get hurt with those things around handy."

"I know. I know. Pinky, if you knew how I suffered just waiting for you to get into port . . ."

"Besides, I haven't hardly any time to do. What would be the sense of asking for a transfer? And besides, what would Captain MacCarven do for a torpedo man? I ask you that. Why, just the other day, he was coming along the deck and he stops where I'm standing there chipping paint and says, 'Davis, you get below and fix up the forward tubes. I can't risk you out here on deck getting sunstroke.' That's what he says to me. How could I leave a guy like that flat?"

Madge leaned her head back against the lattice and looked up at the sky. "I don't mean to whine, Pinky. I don't want you to worry about me any. You go ahead and do what you think is right."

He opened his mouth to speak and then closed it again. A beam of faint light had glittered for a second beneath Madge's eye. "Aw, don't cry, honey. Don't cry like that." He patted her shoulder. "Honest, honey, I feel bad about it too. Listen," he lowered his voice, "I get scared too. I get all weak in the knees every time I hear that water closing in over my head, and I just have to stand there and stare at the bulkhead and hope that nobody notices it. I don't like pigboats any more than you do." His voice jumped a note. "I know how it would feel. I know how it would feel to know that you couldn't ever see the sun again! And that nobody'll ever find you. And you'll rot way down there in the dark water fleeting you about. I know how you get when the water hits the batteries. It did once, and I choked for hours." He was speaking rapidly. "You just sit there for hours letting the green, dirty water creep up, up, up, waiting for it to cut you off. You'd stand on a bunk and press your face against the upper deck trying to get the

41

last breath of air. And maybe you'd hear hammers tapping out Morse right above you. And you'd run around in circles screaming. And nobody would hear. The forward torpedo room is a trap! If anything ever went wrong down below, they'd slam the hatch shut and let you drown! I know, I was aboard the *S-4* after she was put in dry dock!" His head fell forward into her lap, his cap rolling onto the gravel of the walk. She stroked his hair for a few minutes, not knowing what to say. She had never known Pinky before this moment.

He raised his head and gazed at her. "I guess"—his voice shook a little—"I guess you think I'm a baby, don't you?" He attempted a laugh which broke off sharply. "Tomorrow and two more days and you and I are going to have some fun. We're going to paint the town, kid biscuit, and then on Thursday I'll see MacCarven and get transferred to a destroyer. I've had more time than I need on subs, anyway. And the torpedo game is better on the surface. I'm good at it. I'll do that. What do you say?"

"I'll be the happiest sailor's girl in the world, Pinky. Eight more months and you and I can—"

"Up there in the mountains someplace. Beyond the Coast Range. I got it all figured out. What do you say?"

It was nine o'clock when they drifted along the Plaza listening to a radio in a shoeshine parlor down the street. They hadn't spoken for a long time, for what was there to say? Once more everything was all right in their world. Thursday and this constant worry would be ended.

The bill at the Balboa Theater attracted them, a play about

children. The ticket girl smiled when Pinky bought the tickets, but not so broadly as the doorman. A sailor and his girl.

Inside the darkened house, they found two seats toward the back, isolated and inviting. Pinky folded his cap and thrust it into the band of his pants after folding the Spanish shawl against the back of the seat.

The feature was just starting. The soft music which accompanied the titles throbbed through the house. They squirmed down into their seats. Pinky's hand groped for and found Madge's small, slim fingers. They gazed at each other for a moment, their eyes deep and warm, then they watched the picture.

The movie swept into itself, a mixture of pathos and comedy, blending into their mood. Submarines were forgotten for the moment. A sailor and his girl were at peace with the world.

And then, just in the middle of a humorously pathetic episode, the screen flashed white. Pinky sat bolt upright. Madge held her breath. A premonition gripped them both. The screen darkened again, this time from the rays of a projection lantern. In two-foot letters tragedy glared forth.

ALL OFFICERS AND MEN OF THE
SUBMARINE SJ-9 ARE ORDERED TO
REPORT ABOARD IMMEDIATELY.
CAPTAIN MACCARVEN

The screen whitened again, and then continued the movie. Pinky slumped back into his seat and gazed at the hand he held in his own. Two big tears started out from Madge's eyes.

"Madge! They can't go to sea. They can't. The broken diving rudder hasn't been repaired. I . . . I . . . It's the rest of this month's dives. I remember now, they weren't completed!"

"Maybe they aren't going to sea." Madge stifled a sob and looked at Pinky hopefully.

"Oh, yes, they are. We can't get our extra day unless we complete the dive quota. They're going to sea all right."

A note of laughter from the screen jarred in upon their thoughts. "Come on, Madge. They won't wait for me very long at the dock."

"Oh, Pinky! Can't you miss the boat? No one will ever know you did it on purpose."

"I belong aboard, kid. I've got to go. Come on."

Outside the theater, San Diego had extinguished its lights. Only a few people were left on the streets. A fog had settled down upon the pavement to curl damply around the faded lampposts. Pinky motioned at a sleepy taxi driver. They climbed into the cab.

"The municipal pier, buddy, and step on it!"

The driver swept the sleep from his eyes and slurred away from the curb. The wet asphalt was treacherous. The wheels spun for a moment before they took hold. A block away from the theater, almost a mile from the pier, the taxi driver bolted across an intersection.

There was a sickening crash of breaking glass and crumbling metal. A driver had sped out from a blind corner to hit the cab broadside.

Pinky shook his head to clear it of sound, and felt for

Madge. She raised her head in a moment and stared about her. Then she clutched at Pinky's shoulders.

"You're all right, honey. You're all right."

The crushed door of the taxi swung open and a head thrust itself out of the fog. There was a nickel badge on the cap. "Anybody hurt? Here, let me help you, lady. You ain't cut nor nothin', are you?" Madge thrust her hand in her pocket and stepped through the door onto the pavement. Pinky followed her.

The cab lay at a crazy angle, two of its wheels smashed in. The other car was dripping water from its battered radiator, one of its headlights still burning and pointing up into the air. The cabdriver held a handkerchief over a cut on his face. The other driver was gesticulating angrily. The policeman who had helped Madge from the cab was scribbling something on a damp sheet of paper. Pinky glanced at the wreckage and tugged Madge by the coat sleeve.

"We've got to get out of this. I'll miss the boat."

"Hey!" The policeman stopped writing. "Where you going?"

Pinky grabbed up his soiled white cap from the pavement. "I've got to make a boat, Officer."

"Oh, I've heard that gag before. You're witnesses to this. Stick around; it won't hurt you."

Madge drew away from her sailor. She gingerly pulled her left hand out of her pocket. "See that, Officer? The sailor is taking me to a hospital."

Pinky stared at the hand. Blood was dripping from the palm. "Honey! Why didn't you tell me?"

*The policeman who had helped Madge from
the cab was scribbling something on
a damp sheet of paper.*

"Hush. Is it all right, Officer?"

"Wait a minute. I'll send for the ambulance!"

"No, he's taking me to the naval dispensary at the dock." She gasped, remembering that the dispensary wasn't open at that time of night.

Pinky wrapped a handkerchief around the palm. "Send for that ambulance, Officer, and be damned quick about it." The policeman ran over to a call box on the corner.

"Now's our chance, Pinky! Come on!"

"I don't give a damn whether I miss that boat or not until you get patched up. Understand?" He tied a knot in the handkerchief. "You wouldn't tend to it yourself. Why didn't you tell me?"

Madge was silent. She had begun to think collectedly once more. The nervousness of the shock had left her. Maybe, after all, Pinky would miss his boat. No one would ever know.

In a few minutes an ambulance screamed up the misty street and skidded to a stop. Pinky helped Madge into the back. The hand was soaking the handkerchief with blood. Madge felt a little sick. She held her hand away from the shawl.

At the hospital a doctor and a nurse were routed out. The doctor gazed at the palm for some time. Then he told the nurse to sterilize some needles. "A couple stitches, that's all. Nothing serious. Be all over in a minute. Feel sick?"

Madge shook her head, feeling Pinky's protecting arm slip around her shoulder. Every moment made her realize how much she loved him. Pinky's face bore a worried expression.

"You won't hurt her, Doc? 'Cause if you do . . ."

The doctor shot a look at him. "I'll try not to, old man.

You know that." He smiled. The nurse took the needles out of the steam pan, and broke some thread tubes, extracting the gut with a small pair of pliers.

Madge winced as the iodine burned into her flesh. Pinky's arm tightened about her shoulders. "Don't you dare hurt her, Doc. Understand? Be careful!" The needle gathered up the loose flesh and brought it together. Madge wasn't watching. Her eyes rested on Pinky's face. Pinky was staring at the needle in agony. He muttered over and over that he'd rather have a detonator explode in his hand.

After what seemed years, the nurse patted the last strip of adhesive into place. The doctor had left the room. "The doctor said to tell you there wouldn't be any charge." She smiled and began to gather up the needles. "That's all."

"Madge, we've still got a chance to make that boat!" He helped her into her coat and they started toward the door. Then Pinky turned and drew a dollar bill from his breast pocket and threw it onto the steam table. The nurse had gone.

The damp air outside bit into their lungs. It had smelled sickishly sweet in the hospital. The street was dark and empty of cars. Somewhere in the fog a streetcar rang its bell. They walked down the steps and onto the sidewalk. Madge was trembling.

Pinky looked at her. "Feel sick?"

"Naw!"

A taxi caught up with them before they reached the car line. They climbed in and as Madge sat back into the corner, she had to fight to keep black from settling across her eyes. Pinky sat on the edge of the seat.

"I wonder if they've shoved off yet." He glanced at a clock which glowed faintly through the mist.

"Honey, can't you stay here?"

"God, Madge, you don't know how rotten I feel about it. I can't. I've got to go. They might need me."

"They'd never know that you knew."

"No. But I'd know."

The cab swept onto Broadway. One of the wrecked cars still lay against the curb.

"All right, honey. You know best." Madge rolled down a window and let the cold air whip at her face. She was feeling sick.

Pinky sat back in the seat and put his arms around her. "Listen, kid. I won't be gone long. Only a couple days. And when I come back we'll have all the fun we had been meaning to have. We'll go out to Balboa Park and feed the pigeons, and take a trip up to La Jolla, and Sunset Cliffs. You can wait two days, can't you? It'll only be seventy-two hours at the most. As soon as we get back, I'll transfer."

"That'll be eternity, dear."

"I wonder if they've shoved off yet. They wouldn't wait for just me. Madge, I feel rotten about it!"

The cab was nearing the end of Broadway. The municipal pier reached out of the fog unexpectedly close. The taxi swung alongside the gangway. A motor sailer was chugging softly against the float. Madge drew a quick breath. It was not too late. Pinky pressed a dollar bill into the driver's hand and told him to wait. Then he helped Madge out of the cab and steadied her as she walked down the gangway.

The motor sailer was filled with silent men. A chief was walking up and down the float.

"Oh, there you are! Come on, get in. Snap into it!" Then he saw Madge and smiled.

She got a little panicky and clung about her sailor's shoulders. "I don't want you to go! I don't want you to go! Oh, Pinky!"

"Listen, honey, I'll be back here before my seventy-two hours are up. Honest I will. Right here on this dock!"

"I'll be waiting, Pinky. Right here, when your boat comes in." Pinky kissed her.

Down the dock, into the boat with its silent men. And away from the dock to be swallowed by fog and darkness. A ship's bell rang out across the water. Madge groped through the mist and sat down upon a box, holding her throbbing hand, and staring out across the shrouded harbor. The Spanish shawl was slipping to the wet planks.

The Drowned City

Chapter One

WHEN I first broached the idea to young Jim Frazer he almost jumped out of his skin. He was sitting on the edge of the bed tying his shoes, and he looked up, his jaw slack.

"Aw," he said, "you're trying to kid me."

I wish now that I had been kidding him, the way things turned out. But I was so enthusiastic about how things had stacked up that I was blind to anything else.

We had just come in from a big salvage job, the two of us. We'd brought home the bacon, all right. Three big chests of it, full of currency and gold bars. And that afternoon, Bert Sullivan, our former boss, had paid us both off.

Our diving pay was considerable. He paid us sixty an hour spent underwater, and he'd given us a tenth of the net profit. All told I had in the neighborhood of fifty thousand bucks just itching to be spent. And that amount of money in the pocket of a deep-sea diver is rarely in place for long.

But this time I didn't have a spree in mind. I wasn't satisfied with fifty thousand. I wanted three or four million at least. And I thought I had come across the right way to pick up that money.

"No," I told young Frazer, "I'm not kidding you. I think

I know where we can rake in a good-sized chunk of money. I'm tired of seeing my bosses get rich on my work."

"So'm I," stated Frazer, "but that doesn't tell me anything. Did you locate a chart of a sunken galleon or something?"

"Not quite," I said. "A sunken city, this time."

"Aw, that's an old gag. A sunken city, humph! They've tried and tried to locate something at Port Royal, Jamaica, and there isn't any use of our sinking our good dough into a thing like that."

"I'm not talking about Port Royal," I told him. "I'm talking about another town. One that you never even heard of."

He blinked at that one because Jim Frazer thought he had run across almost anything you could name. He had been in the diving game and salvage racket for about three years, and so far he'd come out pretty lucky. On this last job he was the one that located the sealed strongroom of the liner. It takes real nerve to plod around in the dark under the sea, but let me tell you, that kid had it.

But although Frazer had been the one to locate that gold, he had received a very small share, due to the fact that he was the junior diver on the job. I was senior to him and got more out of it. But Frazer didn't hold that against me. He held it against old Sullivan, and rightly. Sullivan was a tightwad if one ever existed.

The town I had in mind was Jamestown, St. Kitts. It went under the waves about 1608 during a hurricane and tidal wave, and it's down there yet. Killed off all the people and destroyed most of the records. There were a couple of government communications which were sent out a few days before the storm hit, and these were the things which had aroused my interest. I'd seen them years ago while in England, and I'd been thinking about it and keeping it under my hat ever since.

I don't care who knows about it now because—well, I'll come to all that later on.

Frazer was interested right away. "How do you know there's any gold down there?"

"I didn't see any bulletins on it," I told him, "because no bulletins have ever been published. Not two people in a million have ever even heard about Jamestown, St. Kitts. Not one person in a hundred million. But I figure it out this way. There were churches down there, and where there were churches in those days you would always see a stack of gold plate and gold cups."

"That's a long shot," said Jim.

"Yes, I admit that that part of it is a long shot. But I happen to know that two British ships scuttled a flotilla of the Spanish Plate Fleet. And these two Britishers, with all that booty aboard, were in that harbor when it happened."

"But you won't find anything like that," he protested.

"Not the ships, we wouldn't. But how about this? I know how they built towns in those days, see? And they would have moved that stuff off those ships and to shore for shipment to England. The gold would be found in a warehouse."

Right about then, if I remember right, we heard a knock on the door, and when the kid opened it, there was Bert Sullivan, fat and greasy as usual, standing there eyeing us.

"What's up?" he wanted to know. "You ain't leaving me, are you?"

Frazer gulped and stared down at the floor. Sullivan thought he had made a diver out of Frazer, when the fact is that Frazer was my protégé. Sullivan read the answer on Frazer's face.

"What?" bellowed Sullivan. "You're going to pull out and leave me flat on my back? We got three contracts that have been hanging fire ever since we've been gone. What'll I do for divers?"

My temper always was sort of bad, I guess. But it got me, having Sullivan talk that way to Frazer after all Frazer had done for him on this last job.

I stepped forward. "Leave the kid alone, Bert. If he wants to quit, that's his business."

"After all I done for him, too!" cried Sullivan, slobbering.

"You never did anything for him," I said. "And he did plenty for you."

"And I suppose you're quitting, too?" growled Sullivan. "Well, get this, Rankin, you won't get any other work around this waterfront after I'm through with you. You can't run out and leave me like this." He shook his big fist under my nose. "And if you ever—"

I don't know what he was going to say. I let him have it. We never got along very good, anyway. He always worked a diver to death—and he'd killed a couple through carelessness and punk equipment. Anyway, I let drive and caught him right on the end of the nose.

He staggered back, swearing. Frazer tried to catch my arms, but the things Sullivan was saying weren't exactly love words, and I don't let that go by any time. I waded into him again.

He kept backing up toward the wall, fending with his forearm and reaching into his hip pocket with his left. He started to whine for mercy, and then, like a sap, I stepped back and let my arms drop to my sides.

A small automatic popped into his hand. I never knew he carried a gun before. He trained the muzzle right on my chest and squinted down the notch along the slide.

"Now I got you!" he roared. "I been waiting a long time for this, Rankin. I'm sick and tired of your damned bellyaching about the equipment and about the dives." His finger started to squeeze down on the trigger.

I stood there like I was paralyzed. I couldn't move. I knew what a gun could do to a man, and when you've seen that effect a few times, you get it in your head that guns are dangerous. I thought sure he was about to drill me, and I guess he would have.

Frazer's foot shot out and hit Sullivan's knuckles. The gun flew up and fell over on the bed. Frazer kicked out again and caught Sullivan in the shin, doubling him up like a jackknife blade.

Somehow the reaction made me feel like laughing. But I was too busy for that right then. I took Sullivan by the coat collar and shot him out of the room. The last I saw of him in New York, he was running as hard as he could go, straight down the hotel corridor, yowling like thirty dozen sharks and a couple barracudas were after him.

"That," said Frazer, "is the last we'll have to do with that old buzzard."

I wish the kid had been right.

Chapter Two

THE trick of finding and fitting out a ship is more difficult than you would think at first. While there are thousands of ships, to find one just right is a hard job. They may look seaworthy and well cared for, but you're likely to find out that the one that seems best actually laid at the bottom alongside a dock for some time. Or it strained every plank in a hurricane. Or it needs to go on the ways for caulking. Or its masts are ready for the woodpile. Or its suit of sails hasn't been aired for a couple of years and is, therefore, moldy and ready to fall apart at the first touch of wind.

Price, in a matter like that, means nothing. Nor do looks, strangely enough. Paint can be wielded by anybody, but only a master craftsman can build a solid, graceful hull.

You see, we had a hard time ahead of us, and we knew it. We were going down into the West Indies in August, and that meant that we would hit the middle of the hurricane season right on the nose. You know what that means. I once saw a five-mast schooner that had come through a blow under ballast down off Puerto Rico. There were five hills in her deck. Five distinct waves fore and aft like a marcel in some sheik's hair. Must have taken some little wind to do that.

But we found a ship. A two-mast auxiliary schooner of

about three hundred tons. At one time there had been a third mast, but it was unstepped, and with the Diesels, we didn't need it. Her name was *Clarabelle,* and we let it stay at that. After we got her all fixed up, we found that she had set us back only a little more than ten thousand dollars. And that's cheap in anybody's money.

The crew was harder than the boat. As soon as I started to stick my long beak around the docks, people knew that something was up. And when we tied the *Clarabelle* up to a wharf, we had to keep a guard on duty twenty-four hours a day to keep the crowds off the deck.

I never did like publicity very much. Oh, this sort's all right, because I can tell the story my own way without decorations. But the newspaper guys always get things in reverse gear, and then ask for more. I never saw the like of it. Two days after we bought the *Clarabelle,* no less than a dozen reporters were barking their knuckles on my cabin trying to get the lowdown. I told them to scram, and they did. It wasn't a wise thing to do, because they wrote the story anyway. Maybe you remember. It ran something like this:

TWO LOCAL DIVERS
HIT TREASURE TRAIL

Harry Rankin and Jim Frazer, known for their salvage exploits in merchant circles, tonight stated that they were after big money in an entirely new locale.

Details were meager, as they stated they "did not want a horde following them in every available canoe." They have posted guards on their ship, the *Clarabelle,* due to the crowds which have been—

The rest of it isn't important. But I figured that the cat was out of the bag, and I was sore. I had a hunch that all wouldn't go well from that minute on, and I was right.

I had to make a flying trip to Washington to get a lot of British Admiralty charts and to buy some hydrographic charts. Also, to get the letters of consent from several embassies. I got them without any trouble and grabbed the first plane back to New York, arriving there shortly after dark.

All the way up I noticed that a man hid his face in back of a newspaper. Once I caught him watching me. Made me feel a little uneasy, because I knew the lengths to which men would go when they thought they smelled gold.

When I got off the plane I went around the field administration building instead of through it. This man followed me, and he was the only one who did out of all the passengers. I got sore.

We reached a particularly unlighted spot, and I turned around and waited for him. He ran straight into me, and I grabbed his lapels.

"What the hell's the idea?" I demanded.

He snorted and stepped away from me. Suddenly I saw a fist coming. But I was ready for it. He sank one punch into my middle and I was short of breath. Then he landed another under my ear and made my head spin.

Taller than I, he looked like a mountain falling on me every time he hit. I gave ground slowly. I couldn't fight with my arms full of charts, so I dropped them. After that the fight was more equal. Suddenly I got the idea that he wasn't trying to hit me so much as he was trying to drive me away.

My right fist slammed his head back twice. Then I caught him in the chest with a terrific wallop. He staggered, and I let up for a split second. But that was long enough.

Before I could move, he had turned around, picked up my charts, and had headed at a dead run through the gate toward the cab line. I sprinted in pursuit, but it wasn't any use. About ten cabs were pulling away from there, and he might have been in any one of them.

Boiling mad, I went straight down to the river to find Jim Frazer. He was there in his cabin, lying in the bunk, looking pretty sick.

When I came in he grabbed for a gun hanging on the wall, but he laid it down when he saw who it was.

"Did you get the charts?" he demanded.

"Yes and no," I said. Then I saw that he had a black eye. "What happened to you?"

Frazer grinned. "Had a little scrap. Nothing much. Heard a noise down in the hold and went down to investigate. Guy jumped on me with all four feet and then got away. He left a few teeth strewn around down there."

"Did he do anything?"

"Not quite," said Frazer. "But he was opening the seacocks when I got there. We would have sunk right here at the dock. Somebody don't want us to go, I guess."

I told him what had happened to the charts. "But," I finished, "I've got the letters I went after, and I guess we can get plenty of charts up here anyway."

"Gee!" cried Frazer, swinging down. "He got the charts?"

"Yes," I said. "He got the charts. But they won't do him any good."

"Who says they won't?" cried Frazer. "Listen. You got a general sheet of the Caribbean, didn't you? And separate sheets of both St. Kitts and Nevis. And another of the harbor at Charlestown, showing the passage and Hurricane Hill."

"Good Lord!" I breathed, a sudden light dawning. "Whoever it is knows right where we're going, and it won't take him five minutes at any public library to find out where we're headed."

"Sure enough!" Frazer leaned back and grinned. "Looks like we're going to have a tough time of it after all. It'd be tough enough, even without opposition."

The next morning I bought some other charts and we looked over the crew for the last time. We had three black boys, a Swede I'd known for a long time, and two Irishmen who had been my "bears" on a job long ago. The cook was a baldheaded wharf rat who talked with a cockney accent, and who claimed to be half-Indian. But he could cook, and that was all we wanted.

At ten, the agent came down with our clearance papers and I paid the bill. At eleven we were all ready to sail. I sent "Bingo," a big black man, down to loosen up the hawsers. Frazer was below, coaxing the Diesels. But before we pulled the plank, who should appear at the bottom but Sullivan. I let him come aboard.

"Well, well," said Sullivan, smiling. "I see you're going for a trip. Did the papers have it right?"

"Wouldn't you like to know!" I said.

He shook his head, making his jowls shake. "Don't be that way. If you're going away, that's that. I came down this morning to make peace with you. Listen, Rankin, I need two divers, and I need them bad."

"What for?"

"To salvage a tramp off Hatteras. Good money in it, too." He pulled at his underlip. "Sure you aren't interested?"

"Nope."

"Well, listen, Rankin, you might at least tell me where I can get two other boys. I always treated you right, and I don't want hard feelings to crop up."

I studied his face and then grinned. "Okay, Sullivan. You can get The Rat and his pal Eddie if you want them. Saw both of them this morning."

"Those two bums?" snorted Sullivan. "I wouldn't have them around!"

"Well, they're all you'll get. There isn't another good diver within a hundred miles who is out of a job. You can't pick all the time, you know."

Sullivan held out his hand. "All right, Rankin. But I hate to lose you boys. I'll even double your pay and share if you'll come back."

"Not us," I said. "Be seeing you, Sullivan." I let go his big paw and he ambled down the gangway.

Twenty minutes later we were heading out for the sea with everything forgotten but the possible gold hoard down in Jamestown, St. Kitts, three centuries below the waves.

We headed for Bermuda, not intending to stop there, but

because you have to go way out in the Atlantic if you expect to angle back and get the trades at 31 degrees or 32 degrees north latitude. We spotted Gibbs Light on the fourth day out, which is some traveling. We went around Bermuda like it was an airplane pylon and bucked into the trades a degree before we expected to hit them.

After that, we set our teeth, heeled hard over, and went roaring down to the Caribbean, every rag taut. The deck, on a ten-degree slant, was as steady as a billiard table. The wind in the sails held it there. In spite of racing waves, the *Clarabelle* stayed there like a painted ship. There was no jarring her once she had her teeth set in that wind.

There's nothing like sail, nothing like a steady helm under your hands, nothing like a set of white wings tight above you against a tropical sky. The ship's a live thing under your feet, vibrant with speed and power. As fleet as a whippet, as thoroughbred as a high-strung horse. The *Clarabelle*—Lord rest her bleaching bones—was a lady.

I got a real thrill out of that cruise because I was master of a vessel for the first time in my life. You see, three hundred tons or under does not require a master's certificate, and we had taken full advantage of that fact. I hate the gross arrogance of a sailing captain underway, and we had purchased a small ship just to avoid that one thing.

We cracked past Barbuda to the north and picked up St. Kitts in the same afternoon. With the trades right at our back, the keel barely touched the waves. We wanted to stop right there in the passage between St. Kitts and Nevis, but we could not. We had to put in to Basseterre, St. Kitts, according to our clearance papers, and we thought that we had better get it over with as quickly as possible.

We spent that night ashore in Basseterre, glad of a bed which was wider than two feet. The hotel was a small two-story structure. The lobby was more a bar than anything else, and up until midnight, a mechanical piano banged strident music into the sweltering night. The last thing I remember was watching the moon's path creep across the floor.

And the next recollection has to do with the sun sweeping in through the glassless window and sizzling my bare feet. I sat up and reached for the pitcher of water on the stand beside the bed. Taking a deep drink, I looked out at a fountain playing in the courtyard against the setting of dark green trees. The tiles, I recall, were yellow and red. A black girl came up with a basket on her head and stooped to drink without removing the load.

Smiling, I turned away, and instantly felt the smile freeze on my face. The transom had been closed the night before to keep out the passage light. It gaped open now.

Below it, embedded deep in the floor, was a sailor's open clasp knife. It had passed all the way through the grass mat and into the planks. I had to pull hard to remove it.

A slip of paper was attached to the blade. Cheap paper on which mammoth letters had been scrawled:

HARRY RANKIN.
KEEP AWAY FROM HURRICANE HILL.
OTHERWISE YOUR DEATH WILL GIVE
US GREAT PLEASURE.

Nothing more than that. I stepped to the window and looked out at the sparkling blue Caribbean. It was as serene as a jewel facet. The town beside it seemed to sleep.

But I could also see the channel entrance far to the south. The entrance where Jamestown had disappeared three centuries before. The note said that death awaited us there.

Well, we could only walk forward in our lead shoes and copper helmets and take what Neptune gave us.

Chapter Three

A BOUT eleven o'clock that morning we were preparing to get underway once more. The cockney-Indian cook had attended to the re-provisioning, and Bingo had climbed over the side early enough to attend to the details of filling all tanks. Everyone was tense with excitement.

I was standing up on the quarterdeck, watching the clouds for possible weather signs, when I heard something scrape against the side. Looking down, I beheld a little cockleshell rowed by a black oarsman. A lank Englishman snatched at our Jacob's ladder and swarmed up the side. He dusted his whites when he reached the deck. Then he removed a sun helmet and wiped the inside of the sweatband with a silk polka-dot handkerchief. Spotting me, he came up the two steps to my level and approached, clearing his throat.

"I beg your pardon, but I fancy I address Mr. Harry Rankin. Is that correct?"

I assured him that it was, with some amusement. That was the last smile I had for some time to come.

"I represent the crown," said the Englishman, tweaking his mustache and regarding me with watery eyes.

He lifted his hat and then wiped it again. I could see that he had something on his chest which was burning at him. Finally, after several weather comments and polite questions about how we had left business in the United States, he came out with it.

"I . . . er . . . have been ordered, Mr. Rankin, to forbid you to search for treasure off Hurricane Hill."

"I'm sorry," I replied, "but I'm busy just now. We're getting underway."

"Then," said the Englishman, "in the name of the king, I demand that your clearance papers be turned over to me immediately for cancellation."

"I know," I said, "that this is Britannia's ocean, but it so happens that this is a United States ship. Get the hell over the side."

Once his foil became engaged, there was no stopping him. "Sir," he cried, "do you realize that we can have you interned here under grave charges? The government forbids any search for treasure without a special order guaranteeing that fifty percent of the total gain be given the crown. All treasure garnered must be turned over to the government for accounting."

"And how long does this process take?"

"Scarcely more than a year."

I laughed in his face. "It's my turn to beg your pardon. But it happens that I am in a slight rush. Sorry to see you leaving us so soon."

"You are insolent," he stated, fuming and sputtering. "It will be my solemn duty to order out a warship to picket you. That is the only way we can guarantee that the crown will benefit by your search."

"We do all the work and you guys get all the dough. That it? Do you realize that it may cost fifty percent of the take to get that stuff out of there? And do you think we're going to work for nothing?"

"I know nothing of these things," snapped the Englishman. "If you do not agree to this, I cannot allow you to leave the harbor."

He seemed to think he owned both harbor and ship. I got sore. He wasn't very heavy, but when I grabbed hold of his coat collar, his weight was almost sufficient to choke him to death. Or maybe it was his wrath which choked him. I'll never know. As gently as possible I dropped him into his boat. In the same motion I waved for Bingo to weigh anchor.

We were out of that harbor before he was even close to the shore.

We beat our way down against the wind toward the passage and Hurricane Hill. *Clarabelle* could go within two points of a breeze, and she was doing it now. We slid around the bottom of St. Kitts and picked up Nevis in the same breath. There wasn't enough room here to tack, and we had to start up the Diesels to swing into our anchorage.

Frazer turned a sextant sideways and sighted on a point of land. "We're almost there," he said.

"And we'll have to work fast," I told him. "Whoever it is that wants to scare us off is trying to do a good job of it. And if we make it before they can get on the scene, we'll still be lucky to get out of the way before a British man-o'-war bears down on us."

"You think they would?" said Frazer. "Seems kind of funny that they'd start acting up like that now when they were so nice to you in Washington. Didn't they receive your letters ashore?"

"Sure they did. But a government isn't better than its people, and its people sure make a habit of changing their collective minds. They, all of a sudden, got the idea that we were after heavy sugar, and the king and crown don't intend to be left out of it by any means. After all, Jim, this is their water, you know."

Frazer made a quick calculation of his sight and then waved the helmsman to the port. We cut onward for a cable length and then straightened out again. Bingo stood up in the bow alongside a winch waiting to let the anchor go to glory.

In spite of the wind, the water was a blue glass sheet below us. Up to this point it had been without shadow—just an azure monotone. I hadn't expected to see anything from the surface, but when I stepped over to the rail to take a sight forward, a shivering rectangle of black far below caught my eye.

There were other squares, other patterns down there. With a shout I held up my hand and let it drop. Bingo sizzled the chain through the hawse. The anchor smashed the water. Our impetus carried us all the way around a circle until we were again facing the west.

"Hey," yelled Frazer, "the sight isn't right yet."

"Maybe not. But I can see buildings down there from right where we're at! This isn't going to be more than a ten-fathom dive!"

Bingo looked into the water and grinned, his white teeth flashing against his ebony face. He was already counting up his share on his fingers, a hundred thousand to each digit.

Frazer took a coin out of his pocket and flipped it up. "Heads I go, tails you take the first dive."

The coin rolled under a steering cable, and we had to get down on our knees to see it. It was heads.

I called for the two Irishmen that we'd nicknamed "Pat" and "Mike." But they were busy at the lockers already, pulling out copper plates and lead belts and twill suits. A black boy was pulling the pump out of its chest and setting it up beside the rail. The Swede was singing some sailor song while he lowered a ladder over the side and fastened its hooks into the gunwale.

In tropical waters you don't use heavy diving underwear. It isn't necessary, because the sea is fairly warm if you don't go too deep. And neither do you use hand lamps, because the sun is bright and the water is clear, and you can see at a hundred feet without any trouble.

Frazer sat down on a three-legged stool and his bears went to work on him. They stripped him and then pulled the diving suit to his waist. He stood up while they laced the legs up the back. Then he sat again and they put the shoes on him. Sixteen pounds apiece those shoes weigh. And the belt is full of lead which weighs about eighty pounds. They screwed down the corselet over his shoulders, and he was all ready for the helmet. I put that on him myself.

We didn't have a telephone cable with us because in clear

water it isn't actually necessary. And we didn't think we'd get into any tangles that a hand-line signal couldn't take care of. We were wrong about that.

While I helped Frazer over the side I saw a flash of light over on St. Kitts. I stopped and waited for it to happen again, but it didn't. I figured that it was just some native swinging a machete. A bright blade will hurl the sun a long way.

Frazer went down the ladder, slow and easy, and then the water closed in over the top of his helmet, and all I could see was his shadow against the white sand bottom and a stream of silver bubbles breaking on the surface.

While I waited for some signal from below I watched St. Kitts. The hand pump was gasping behind me and the bubbles were still coming up. Bingo was chattering with excitement under the spanker mast.

Once more I saw that flash of light from the knoll. I couldn't be sure what it was. Evidently one of the Irishmen had also seen it. He pushed a pair of binoculars into my hand. Spinning the setscrew I scanned that knoll top.

For a while I didn't see anything. These two islands were once one and the distance is not great between them. The tidal wave that took Jamestown down below also separated the strip of land.

I saw something move in a tree. Thinking it was a man I watched it for some time. Then I knew that it was a monkey. There's a whole tribe of those things on the two islands, and they all run together. Some of the natives hunt them. In Basseterre I'd been told that these monkeys were seen only on one of the islands at a time. Either St. Kitts or Nevis.

The funny part about that is that monkeys can't swim, and they certainly don't use boats. How, then, could they travel from one island to the other? Later I found out how they did.

I tired of watching the monkey and swung the glasses down closer to the ground examining the underbrush. Pretty soon the light flashed again. I spotted it that time and watched. Then I realized what it was.

A man was lying under a bush. And the flash of light came from the lenses of the field glasses he was using! We were being watched!

That made a shiver run down my spine. If it was the government, they'd come out in a launch. Then, who the devil could it be? The man who had left that knife and note in my hotel room? Was someone actually going to carry out the threat?

I glanced down at the water, but the bubbles were still bouncing up in a little mound. Feeling easier, I checked up on the pressure gauges.

"Better pump a little faster," I told Pat. "He isn't getting enough air."

He raised his bushy brows, and started to spin the brass wheel at about twice the speed.

"Must be a leak in the pump," I decided. "But he can live off that while he's down. We'll fix it after he surfaces."

"Pardon me, sir," said Pat, "but it feels kind of slack to me."

Without breaking the even twist of the wheel, I took it over. It did feel slack. However, that might have been caused by the pump. You never can tell about these hand outfits. And I don't like motor-driven affairs, either. I had a motor stop on me once when I was down at a hundred and ten feet. They didn't have any auxiliary pump to switch to, and they dragged me out cold. If a man drops, you've always got another man to shove in his place and nothing is lost.

"Bubbles still coming," observed Bingo at the rail. "Reckon he's all right."

Nevertheless, I turned over the wheel and picked up the lifeline. I gave it an easy tug. It met no resistance. I pulled at it again. Still nothing happened. Pulling slowly, so as to keep from dragging Frazer over the sand or off a pinnacle, I started to take in the line. It coiled up at my feet, and the coil grew bigger and bigger. Bingo's eyes were bulging out of his black face. I felt like a sawdust doll—without any strength at all.

Suddenly, both air hose and lifeline flipped out of the water. I stared at them stupidly.

"My Lord!" cried Bingo. "They been—been cut!"

The two dangling ends swung to and fro in the gentle swell.

Chapter Four

THERE wasn't enough daylight left for a dive, nor was there any reason for me to take a dive. If Jim Frazer had been without air for the past five minutes he was dead, and that's all there was to it. I knew that somebody or something had cut his lines long before I had found it out. When the pump had begun to turn easier, Jim Frazer's lines were already severed. I couldn't save him. Not now.

I spent that night pacing the deck, staring out into the gloom, anxious for the sunlight to come again. I didn't want to make a night dive. I owed some kind of a debt to the crew.

When the sea calmed for sunup, the men were ready with my outfit. The fuzzy-faced one we had dubbed Pat wouldn't look me in the eye, and when I started to take off my shoes for the suit, he finally got off what he had been mustering up nerve enough to say.

"I wish you wouldn't go," he said. "I tell you, sir, nobody on this here windbag knows nothing about navigating her. And if anything was to happen to you—"

"You'd be stranded right here, that it? Well, there's nothing going to happen to me, so stop worrying." I picked up a steel and brass rod from the deck at my side. "See this? It's an acetylene torch, and if anybody gets gay with me they'll get the works down there."

"But maybe, sir," replied Pat, "maybe you won't even see 'em before it's too late. Just between you and me, sir, I don't like to see you take the chance. It's my private opinion that you— Beg pardon, sir, but—"

"That you won't ever see me again. That right?"

"Well, not exactly, but—I don't like this a bit. That guy was laying for us over on that knoll yesterday."

"Sure," I said. "But there isn't any boat in sight."

"That's all right, too," said Pat. "But there's such a thing as a self-contained diving suit in which a guy can walk miles over a floor like this. And a ship could hide behind any one of those points of land over there. Not more'n a mile away, they are."

I looked over at St. Kitts and then back at Nevis. We could be attacked from either side. I knew that. But I had to know what had happened to Frazer, and I wanted to at least make a stab at the gold if there was any down there. I couldn't lie down and quit.

The sun came swimming up, a bloody ball, staining the clouds a dull red. To the south some clouds were hanging fire as though waiting to charge us. The air felt heavy and tasted stale. I knew that a storm, perhaps a hurricane, was on its way. That meant I'd have to work fast if I wanted to work at all. If our anchor chains didn't hold, a blow would brush us ashore in no time.

Finally the men got me turned out. I fastened the faceplate on my helmet and clumped over the rail, feeling for the rungs of the ladder, gripping the torch in my left hand. Through the helmet I could hear it burn and sizzle. The lines came reluctantly after me.

The water felt warm around my legs, my waist, my shoulders, and then the suit got light around me as it filled out. Abruptly the world went blue before my face. I was under.

The ladder didn't go more than ten feet, and when I reached the bottom rung I let go, falling like a feather through the murky world. The rays of sunlight were long, slanting streaks all about me.

A fish swam up and looked at me and then went away. The green belly of a shark passed over me. I felt the swirl of his passage. I never worry about sharks because they're harmless unless you corner them. I kicked one in the nose once and he charged me, but now I leave them alone and they leave me alone. A barracuda is the only thing I ever look out for. They tackle anything that moves, and their jaws run better than a quarter of the length of their long bodies. They're faster than light. Not much use to worry about them either, because if one attacks, you rarely see him until he's right there with you, and then it's too late to think about anything.

The sand floated up and hit the underside of my lead shoes. Quite a current was running, and I had to lean forward into it like a man leans into the wind. Then, like a slow-motion picture, I went ahead toward a dark bulk which had housed people three centuries before.

Of course, there was nothing much left of the place but the shattered walls. You could see where a door had been, and while I stood there studying it, I saw a school of fish whisk out of it. Made me feel funny, that sight. Way over to the right two sharks were swimming in a circle, and as I watched them they suddenly turned and bolted away from an object I could not see. I wondered for a moment what had scared them, and then forgot about it. I remembered very vividly a few minutes later.

It was eerie in the world of half-light. The hulks of old stone buildings stood in an orderly row ahead of me. Some of the rocks had tumbled out into the street, partially blocking it. Evidently Jamestown had been built out of lava blocks for lack of lumber. The stones had stood the weathering of the current. The city had been dropped about seventy-five feet and the shock had broken it considerably, but it still looked like a town.

Careful that I didn't tangle my lines, I went down the first block. I had the torch for light, and I looked inside each building. Frazer should have been along there someplace, judging from his bubble track, but I could find no sign of him. In one place the fungus had been scraped off a stone face to expose a chiseled name. I knew he had passed that point, and I went on expecting to see him at any minute.

Sea ferns had grown up through the debris and they waved slowly back and forth in the current as though keeping time to a waltz. Once an octopus scuttled out of a dark corner and zipped past me in a cloud of spraying ink. He had been more startled than I had been.

The half-light was getting me a little. I felt as though someone was standing, hidden, watching me. It was spooky enough without that, and I plunged on, battling the sweep of water, still looking.

At last I came to a jump-off which lay green blue before me. That, I knew, had been the "waterfront." The tumbled remains of a stone quay lay on my left, and behind that stood a collapsed pile which might have been a warehouse at one time. I struggled toward it, suddenly excited. This would be the place they had stored the gold from the British vessels.

I noticed a funny thing about the waterfront. It curved away until it ran almost directly north and south. That meant that a man could walk the sea floor from St. Kitts to Nevis without going down farther than about fifteen fathoms.

Feeling around the warehouse, I discovered a caved doorway. It was necessary to climb over a pile of stone and wiggle through a small opening to get through, but I pulled in some slack on the lines and boosted myself up.

The inside was blacker than pitch. My torch made only a slight dent in the darkness, and I had to look closely to make sure that I wasn't diving off into a hole. Fumbling my way along I finally descended to the bottom. The place had once had a stone floor, but the rocks were mostly upended, making walking a near impossibility.

My torch struck on a patch of bright surface. Crawling over to it I saw that the moss had been stripped away from an ancient brass cannon which was stored there. My heart began to beat rapidly. Jim Frazer had passed this way. I was sure of that. And whatever had gotten him was lying ahead of me there in the dark, ready to pounce on me.

It took all the nerve I could muster and a great deal to spare to carry on through that vault. I couldn't give all my time to watching; I had to look for the gold which had been stored there.

The wall was easy to locate, and I went down it, feeling my way inch by inch. The floor was more solid. In fact, it had the appearance of natural stone. Possibly this section of the warehouse had been constructed on a point of rock.

Ahead of me I saw a dark square on the floor. It was better than ten feet by ten, extending out beyond the limit of my light. I started to step down upon it and then thought better of the move. I reached out with my hand and pressed the surface to make certain that it was perfectly solid. I felt it move!

I knew that I was close upon two things. The gold and the mystery of Frazer's disappearance. And something else. Looking back toward the entrance, I could see no light. I supposed, then, that I had unwittingly turned a corner and thought no more about it.

Once again I pressed the black square. A ripple of current whisked past my palm. It was all out of proportion to the water movement which would have been caused by moving that plate. I was more than mystified. I pushed harder. The resulting sweep of water almost drew me against the square. Drawing back to brace myself, I saw the rectangle slide into place once more.

Squatting on my haunches in the dark, I eyed the thing and thought it over. If a man wasn't careful he'd be carried right into whatever lay below him.

I decided that I would need a rope. Turning, I started to

crawl out toward the door and then stopped. The entrance was lighted again by daylight in the sunken street. This gave me considerable pause, because it meant only one thing. Someone or something had been crawling through that door at the last glimpse.

The acetylene torch threw sparks through the surrounding murk. Above the gurgle of my helmet I could hear nothing. But something was telling me not to move. I was not alone in that vault.

A shadow loomed up at my right and then disappeared again. I shoved the torch high above me and stared. A helmet was there! A diver had come up on me while my back was turned.

For one crazy instant I thought it was Frazer. Then I knew that I was wrong. Frazer couldn't live for sixteen hours without air hoses. This, then, had some connection with the man who had watched from the point.

While I watched, the diver rose up and threw himself at me. It was terrible, the way he floated through space. I started to dodge, but the move was sluggish. His glinting copper helmet looked like a yellow balloon coming at me. Eight inches of steel glittered in his right hand. His left swept down upon the torch.

I squirmed to one side, trying to evade him. His intent was only too clear. He didn't want to run the knife through my body. He wanted to sever my lines. I thanked the Lord for the broken floor at that moment. Otherwise he could have found the only connection I had with sunlight, and in finding it, he could have hacked the hidden hose with one slash.

The steel floated at me. My arm pressed up toward it. Seconds flicked past. Straining against the wall of water all around me was a terrific effort. I tried to shove the torch at his helmet, but he held my arm powerless. If his knife so much as scratched the two layers of twill and one of rubber which encased me, I would be a dead man. Lying as I was, in a horizontal position, the water would rush into my suit and fill my helmet before I could straighten up—providing he would immediately release me, which would not happen. As soon as he had touched me he would follow up his advantage.

The torch wavered close to his faceplate, but not close enough. My arm would not reach that far. All I could do was to keep the knife at bay and try to get up. Suddenly he ceased to push with the knife. I shifted, trying to get an advantage. The move was slow, and before I was even over on the side, his sixteen-pound lead shoe slammed against my legs and he had me in a scissors grip.

A small hose ran from the pack he carried on his back to the helmet. That was his air line going up from the oxygen tank. I dropped the torch and he grabbed for it. But before his fingers touched the rod, I had clamped down on his short hose. I threw my right arm out of his grasp and snatched at the setscrew of the faceplate.

In that instant he realized that the tide had turned. Even if he succeeded in getting my suit with his knife, he, too, would die. Throwing all his strength into one great push he heaved himself back from me, floating upward through the arc lighted murk above us. It was weird seeing him float over me, suspended in "midair."

Then he swooped down again. At first I did not know his intent. I thought that he was trying to get away from me until I saw his knife flash once more. He was diving for my lines!

I pushed myself off the floor and tried to reach him again. One hand caught the acetylene rod and I held it before me like a spear. His knife was bearing down on the rubber air hose. In one split second I would be cut off from my air supply, to die of suffocation.

Tense horror crowded at my throat. To move at all was difficult, and to move swiftly was impossible. It took me five seconds to get within five feet of him. I know, because I counted them into my bubbling helmet.

The torch showed up his face. I had a vague feeling that I knew him, that I had seen him somewhere. But that didn't matter now. Nothing mattered but the effort to keep him from cutting my line. I saw the edge of the knife disappear into the rubber. I saw bubbles shoot up as he cut into the line. The pressure in my helmet was instantly less.

He didn't think I could make it. A vicious grin was visible through his faceplate. The next instant my torch reached him. Sparks flew away from the copper. The blue white jet of flame stabbed through his helmet. Suddenly heated air burst forth.

I slumped back, feeling sick, watching him. The water wouldn't let him fall swiftly. He drifted down to the floor and bumped against the torn rocks strewn there.

Finally, I got up energy enough to crawl toward the irregular space of light. When I had reached it, I looked back at him. He was nothing more than a shadow from which silver bubbles were issuing. A current caught at his arms and made them flop grotesquely.

When I reached the drowned street I looked up to see that the light was failing.

I knew by the tug of the tide and then the uneasy motion of the water that a storm had broken up there. Down below, everything looked serene and quiet. The clusters of tall ferns were waving gently as though touched by a slow, mystic wind.

Chapter Five

MY line held until I reached the surface. I shut off the torch and used both hands to hold the rubber hose together. They had to pull me up by the lifeline.

Coming out of that quiet into the storm was a shock. The waves were running about fifteen feet, and I was almost smashed against the hull before they pulled me in.

Bingo let go the pump when he saw me and heaved a sigh, wiping his black face with a blacker hand. The spattering rain made his naked torso glisten like polished wood.

"Lordy," muttered Bingo. "You had me worried, Mistah Rankin. I never expected to see you again, never. No, suh!"

As soon as Mike got my helmet and corselet off me he said, "We're going to have to step lively. This is only a taste of what's coming, let me tell you. See how black and greasy it is over there in the east. That means hurricane, and nothing else but."

I climbed out of the suit. I didn't have time to acquaint them with the details of my narrow escape on the bottom. There were too many other things to be accomplished. I could see by the shoreline that we had dragged our anchor some little distance. There was nothing to do but start the Diesel and scurry for shelter on the other side of Hurricane Hill, which would afford protection from the blow.

*Coming out of that quiet into the storm was a shock.
The waves were running about fifteen feet, and I was
almost smashed against the hull before they pulled me in.*

Frazer was certainly a gap in our company. His white cap was swinging back and forth in the engine room as we pitched, calling to mind the fact that he had been with us such a short time ago.

After starting the engines I left one of the black boys in charge and went up to take the helm. It took us no time at all to turn. The wind caught in our bow and hurled us about-face in a minute.

The helm was slippery with rain and spray, and the scuppers were running inches deep. I was soaked in no time, and the cloth flapping against my ribs was cold. Water ran out of the brim of my cap and hindered my vision. Otherwise I would have seen the other ship before I did. We might have had a chance to run if I'd located it in time. But I didn't, and it wasn't until the wind was cut off by Hurricane Hill that I spotted the black salvage tug to the lee.

The engines died and we coasted in closer to shore. The salvage tug might have been manned by dead men for all the movement it made. Through the rain I couldn't see very much of it. Just a splotch against the water and sky. It was a tug, I knew. And I also understood that it might be the base of the diver I had killed.

Our anchors rattled out, and we swung our bow into what little wind there was here. We could do nothing now but wait. We knew that the storm hadn't even begun to blow yet, and we busied ourselves with lashing everything down that might shake loose.

Disappointment and rage were all tangled up inside me. I hadn't located any gold, and I hadn't even found Frazer's body. Maybe I was expecting too much in too little time, but all I had managed was to nearly get myself killed.

The next thing I heard about the tug came from Bingo. "Ahoy!" he shouted from the bow. "Look whar you're going!"

A glance showed me that the salvage tug had slid up on us unobserved. Even now she was less than fifty feet off our starboard bow and coming closer each second.

I dived into a cabin and came up with an automatic. When I reappeared, the tug was about to scrape against us. Two wharf rats were holding grappling hooks ready to cast over our rail. It was nothing more than an old pirate trick—locking one vessel to another so that the boarding party could get across without any danger to themselves.

Leaning against the whooping wind and stinging rain, I lifted the gun and shouted: "I'll drill the first man that sets foot on this deck!"

A hulking shadow loomed close to the other's rail. "Put that gun down! I've got ten rifles trained on you this minute!"

I backed off, hesitating. It might be a bluff on his part, but I didn't dare take the chance. There wasn't any use committing suicide.

When the first man hit our deck he landed almost on top of me. I was as nervous as a cat. When he slapped down, he bumped me. He held a revolver. Without thinking, I swung at him with my own gun. He went down like a tenpin.

Somebody yelled over on the other boat. That brought a flood of men over to our deck. In the next instant the planking seemed to be hidden by the rolling, twisting bodies of fighting men. My six were tangling with his dozen.

A big bruiser dived at me. I sidestepped and let him have it between the eyes with the gun butt. He dropped, and before I could turn, a pair of arms came around from behind me and lifted me clear off the deck. I soared through the sheeting rain into the scuppers.

In an instant I was up, scrambling back into the melee, though I knew that it was little use. They had us fair and square. We couldn't escape. I couldn't find the voice to call for quarter, and I never had a chance, anyway. The first thing I knew, two sailors grabbed me and yanked me across the deck to the mast.

Although I kicked and squirmed, they held me there and tied me tight with a halyard. My gun was gone, and my head ached where somebody had clouted me. Besides, I was tired after my long tour on the bottom. There wasn't anything I could do.

One of the Swedes was lying in the scuppers, the water running over his face, washing the blood which seeped from his cracked skull. Bingo was sitting on a hatch rolling his eyes at a gun muzzle which a sailor held on him.

The wind shrieked through the rigging and the rain beat steadily on the deck. I tried to spot the man who was at the head of the gang of cutthroats that had jumped us.

Pretty soon I saw him climb over our rail and waddle up to me. He was grinning and his greasy face was streaked with dirt and rain. His eyes were the size of a pig's, and had just that expression.

I wasn't even surprised when I recognized Bert Sullivan.

"So, it's Rankin," said Sullivan. "Where's your little pal, Frazer?"

A big bruiser dived at me. I sidestepped and let him
have it between the eyes with the gun butt.

"You ought to know," I told him. "Your diver murdered him."

"Yeah? Well, I've got a hunch it was the other way around."

That instant I remembered who the man I had killed was. The guy we used to call The Rat. He was better off dead, anyway.

Sullivan wiped the rain out of his eyes and grinned again. He was getting a kick out of it, I knew. "You'll get off easy, Rankin, if you'll just tell me where you located the gold. If you tell me straight out, I won't do much to you. Otherwise—"

"Otherwise, what?" I snapped.

He reached down and picked up the torch I had dropped when I came aboard. Close by, he found a sparker and lighted it. The acetylene sputtered and crackled in the rain.

He poked it at me playfully. "If you don't come clean about it, we'll have a little roasting party. I'll start on your feet."

I didn't think he had guts enough to go through with it. After all I'd worked with the man, and though he'd been a little cracked about a lot of things, he seemed familiar. He couldn't bluff me, and he knew it.

Sullivan shoved the torch at my feet. It scorched through my canvas sneaks. A white pain shot up the calf of my leg.

"How about it?" he said, still grinning.

I didn't think he'd go any further, and I didn't want to beg for mercy in front of him or in front of my own crew. He stabbed the torch against my other foot. It was agony.

After that he stepped back, watching like a bloated cat.

"The next time," said Sullivan, "I'm going to ram this thing down your throat."

One of his sailors laughed. Bingo rolled his eyes up at the gun. He decided not to chance it.

"I don't know where the gold is," I told him. "All I know is that there might be some there. And that one of your murdering devils—probably The Rat—killed Frazer yesterday afternoon. If you think you can get away with this in British territory—"

Sullivan laughed at that. He knew that it was an empty threat. The British wouldn't care what happened to the *Clarabelle* after that little incident in Basseterre.

"So you didn't find it," said Sullivan.

"No!"

He shrugged. "All right, Rankin. If you didn't, you didn't, and there's no use of my sticking around." He hefted the torch. "But before you trail to hell after The Rat, Rankin, I'd like to give you a little laugh.

"I heard you talking to Frazer in your room. I waited outside the door and heard the works. And then, to make sure, I had a man steal your charts. You're a fool, know that? It was too easy. I made better time down here than you did because I bought me a new tug, see?

"I almost scuttled your ship in New York, but the man bungled the job. I tried to scare you out by dropping you a note in Basseterre, but you're too dumb to know what fear is. Now I'm going to get rid of you, your crew, and go back to look for the gold after this storm is over."

He hefted the torch and stepped closer to me. There was no way out. He was set on killing me. He thought he had a grievance.

The torch was hot against my face. In the next minute it would burn a hole straight through my skull and into my brain. Poetic justice, I thought. The Rat had got his a few hours before with that same torch. But The Rat had been trying to kill me and I wasn't trying to kill anybody.

Abruptly, a shot whanged out from the outboard rail. Splinters flew away from the side of the mast. All eyes jerked in that direction. The man who covered Bingo swung away, raising his gun. A second shot wiped out his face.

A grim-faced fellow started to run toward the source of the bullets. He tripped and fell, dead before he hit the deck.

Sullivan let out a yowl and a command at the same instant. Dropping the torch, he scuttled toward his salvage tug, which banged against the inboard gunwale.

Bingo rose up and took his late captor's weapon to send five rapid shots into the fleeing men. He dropped one.

Mike untied me with shaking hands. I tried to get loose in time to prevent Sullivan getting away, but before I had a chance he had swung off the grappling hooks and the tug was plunging ahead.

The rifle spoke from the rail again. The helmsman of the salvage boat pitched half out of the bridge window and stayed there, arms dangling. Engines wide open, the tug sprinted for the channel.

We were in the shelter of Hurricane Hill. We weren't catching either blow or waves. But out there in the open the gale was shrieking at a hundred miles an hour, and no small boat could survive it.

The tug receded to a shadow in the driving gray of rain.

After that it was gone—forever. Caught by the gale, its decks were stripped. The waves battered it into so much driftwood.

I shuddered when I thought of it. Compared to us, the tug was a strong boat. If we had been caught in that we wouldn't have lasted a split second. As it was, from the evidence picked up later, the tug lasted long enough to launch a boat. The boat, of course, never lived long enough to be manned. It was cast ashore a week later, utterly shattered.

With the tug gone, I turned to the rail to find out the identity of the mysterious benefactor. I almost dropped in my tracks when I saw him.

It was Jim Frazer!

He was leaning on the rifle, grinning at me. I was so glad to see him that, for the life of me, I can't remember what happened for the next half-hour.

When I pressed him for an explanation, he pulled me down into the comparative shelter of a cabin and poured himself a drink.

"It's a long story," he said, "but the meat of it is this. I found a bronze door down in an old warehouse and I thought it was solid. Well, it wasn't. It shot me through like a bullet. Evidently, the thing is hinged from the center both ways and although it's almost watertight, it's so perfectly balanced that the pressure of the sea can't budge it as long as the weight is equal all over the surface.

"Well, when I dropped through, it slammed back shut and severed my lines. I thought I was a goner for a minute. Honest I did. But right away I felt around and, Harry, I wasn't in water anymore!

"All I had to do was to take off my helmet and walk straight ahead. Of course, there was some water on the floor. I'd let that in. But the rest of the tunnel was pretty dry. It was like the Holland Tunnel under the Hudson, except that nature built this one.

"It was there when Jamestown went under the waves, and the drop of the land was so even that it didn't even shatter this hollow passageway under the sea. I walked out, and the next thing I knew, I was on Hurricane Hill.

"Being pretty tired, I took a nap. I tried to signal you, but it was too dark, and a fellow doesn't carry matches in a diving suit. So all I could do was wait. I walked back through the woods and got lost, and when I saw the sea again, the storm broke. I saw you come into this cove, and I found a small boat. Then I saw this other ship attack you. So I went back and dug out a couple of natives. They had a rifle, and I promised them a hundred dollars for it.

"When I came out here, I guess the surprise was too much for them. I shot, hanging onto the Jacob's ladder, and they could hardly see me. They must have thought I was a couple dozen—maybe a British patrol.

"Anyway, Harry, here I am. And I guess we've proved the story of the monkeys appearing on one island at a time, but never both at once. And that isn't all we've proved."

"What's that?" I said.

"I found the treasure down in that tunnel. Before Jamestown sank, that place was the official safe."

Well, that was all there was to that. After the blow we went back through the tunnel and pulled the stuff out. We didn't

97

have any trouble at all. Except with the British. They sent their warship out the next day, and we had to turn the stuff over to them.

Frazer and I have been getting along okay, though things have been pretty lean for the last six months. The accounting of the gold won't come up until after the first of the year.

I am not at liberty to state the amount of the treasure. And I don't think I could, anyway. It was more than we could both carry in twenty trips into the tunnel, and it wasn't just gold, either. However, the British are getting all that straightened out for us.

Before I stop, I want to remark that if I hadn't happened to sell this story of our little jaunt, we wouldn't be eating right now. But when that accounting comes up, we've got plans for a spree!

Story Preview

Story Preview

NOW that you've just ventured through some of the captivating tales in the Stories from the Golden Age collection by L. Ron Hubbard, turn the page and enjoy a preview of *Under the Black Ensign*. Join Tom Bristol as he barely escapes an unjust death sentence aboard the British HMS *Terror* when the ship is overtaken by pirates. Soon enough, Bristol is stranded on a desert island for stopping a pirate mutiny. When Lady Jane Campbell joins Tom at sea, things really set sail in this swashbuckling adventure.

Under the Black Ensign

"YOU blackguard! You insolent whelp!" shouted the governor. "Trying to murder me? 'Od's wounds, what have you to say for yourself?"

"My marline—" Bristol began, his voice quite steady.

"Shut up!" cried the governor. "It's attempted murder, that's what it is! Attempted murder! You're in the pay of France to kill me. I see how it is now. I see how it is!"

Captain Mannville, his arrogant face rimmed by a silvery beard, stared holes into Bristol. "We've had trouble with you before, my man. You realize, of course, that your act will not pass without punishment."

Bristol glanced at the others. Their faces were fat and red with soft living, but for all that, the hardness there, those merciless eyes, had sent many a sailor groveling to the deck before them.

Not that this was a particularly cruel set of officers. Perhaps they were even more kindly than the average of the Royal Navy. But this was 1680, and the tide of lust for empire had swung high in the great nations of the world. Human life was nothing. Compassion was almost forgotten. Britain was setting herself to rule the seas, and Spain was setting the example for bestiality.

The Lord High Governor—late of the London courts, where he had been Sir Charles Stukely, gentleman-in-waiting to the King—planted his feet wide against the persistent annoyance of a swinging deck and breathed hard, as though trying to stifle ungentlemanly wrath.

"Flogging takes it out of them," said Sir Charles. "If we let this insult pass, God knows the results upon the rest of this mangy scum."

Captain Mannville nodded. "Ah, yes. Flogging. Bristol, stand to the mast and prepare yourself for a hundred lashes."

Bristol's steadiness deserted him. He stepped back, found the rail, and supported himself with it. His face was a little gray through his dark tan. The brisk trade wind was in his light brown hair, ruffling it.

"A . . . a hundred lashes, sir? My God, it's death!" Through his mind ran the scenes of other floggings. Thus far he had escaped that ever handy cat-o'-nine, used in all navies to maintain discipline. No man had lived through a hundred lashes.

"A hundred lashes!" cried Sir Charles. "Perhaps that will teach the fool to respect the persons of his betters. That murderously thrown belaying pin might have snuffed out my life!"

A marlinespike is hardly a belaying pin. Something in the remark gave Bristol strength. After all, he, Tom Bristol, was a sailor, and this Sir Charles was a landlubber. The contempt possessed by all sailors came to Bristol's aid.

Pushing himself away from the rail and standing up straight, he looked the Lord High Governor in the eye. "It happens, sirrah, that the marlinespike fell quite by accident. But had I known that it would fall, I am certain that I would have pitched it more accurately."

Sir Charles' face became dangerously purple again. He grew in size, his fat width puffed out, his voice broke through the bonds of his rage.

"You . . . you address me as 'sirrah'? You intimate that . . ." He was speechless. His eyes threatened to pop out on his cheeks.

"Silence, Bristol!" said Captain Mannville. "For that insolence you shall receive an additional hundred lashes."

Bristol turned on him. His eyes were reckless now. There was something wild and vibrant about him as he stood there, like a fine steel blade quivering.

"A hundred lashes more?" cried Bristol, almost laughing. "I'll be dead in the first seventy-five! And while I'm still able to talk, Mannville, there's something I have to say which might interest you."

"Silence!" cried Mannville, his hand on the butt of his pistol.

"Go ahead and shoot! The quicker the better!"

Bristol was aware of faces outside the circle. Men of the crew were staring at him, unable to believe that anyone would have the courage to speak thus to *gentlemen*.

"Five months ago," said Bristol, "I went ashore in Liverpool. Before I even entered a tavern, I was set upon by your press gang and dragged out to this ship. When I tried to protest, you had me thrown in irons.

"Mannville, it has never made any difference to the Royal Navy who manned its men-o'-war. In my home port, I am listed as dead. My ship sailed without me.

"Press ganging may have some justification when applied to men on the beach, but it happened, Mannville, that I was first mate of the bark *Randolph* out of Maryland."

"Silence!" cried Mannville again. He was having some difficulty looking this man in the eye, and that fact did little to improve his temper.

"I demand that this insolent wretch be punished instantly!" bellowed the Lord High Governor. "First he tries to murder me, and then he dares to speak this way to officers of the King!"

Mannville stepped back and made a sign to two British Marines. They fell upon Bristol and carried him swiftly to the mast. Two lines were ready there for any man who might be unlucky enough to be flogged. These were immediately made fast to Bristol's wrists.

Facing the mast, his arms drawn above him painfully tight, he felt the hot sun on his bare back. He saw the quartermaster step forward. In the quartermaster's hand was the cat-o'-nine.

Originally the cat-o'-nine-tails was merely a collection of thongs held together in a short handle. But the Royal Navy had changed all that. This cat-o'-nine had brass wire wound about the ends of the thongs, and the brass was tipped by pellets of lead.

Wielded by brawny quartermasters, the cat-o'-nine was responsible for more deaths than scurvy or gunshot.

The captain stepped back. Sir Charles moved a little closer.

The Lord High Governor's eyes were brittle hard, like polished agate.

The lash went back with a swift, singing sound. Bristol clenched his teeth and shut his eyes, expecting the white-hot flash of pain.

To find out more about *Under the Black Ensign* and how you can obtain your copy, go to www.goldenagestories.com.

Glossary

STORIES FROM THE GOLDEN AGE *reflect the words and expressions used in the 1930s and 1940s, adding unique flavor and authenticity to the tales. While a character's speech may often reflect regional origins, it also can convey attitudes common in the day. So that readers can better grasp such cultural and historical terms, uncommon words or expressions of the era, the following glossary has been provided.*

Aboukir Bay: inlet of the Mediterranean Sea lying near the mouth of the Nile along the coast of Egypt.

Alexandria: the second largest city in Egypt and its largest seaport, extending about twenty miles along the coast of the Mediterranean Sea in north central Egypt.

anchorage: that portion of a harbor, or area outside a harbor, suitable for anchoring, or in which ships are permitted to anchor.

arc light: a lamp that produces light when electric current flows across the gap between two electrodes.

Asia Minor: the peninsula of western Asia between the Black Sea and the Mediterranean Sea. Throughout history Asia Minor has served as a crossroads for migrating peoples and a battleground for competing Asian and European civilizations.

auxiliary: describes a boat with an engine to supplement or replace the sails.

Balboa Park: a 1,200-acre urban cultural park in San Diego, California. Besides open areas and natural vegetation, it contains a variety of museums, theaters, gardens, shops and restaurants, as well as the renowned San Diego Zoo. Among its gardens is the Japanese Friendship Garden that first opened in 1915.

ballast, under: a ship carrying no cargo, only ballast. *Ballast* is any heavy substance, as stone, iron, etc., put into the hold to sink a vessel in the water to such a depth as to prevent capsizing.

bark: a sailing ship with three to five masts.

batteries: groups of large-caliber weapons used for combined action.

battlewagon: battleship.

"bears": from the phrase "come bear a hand," which means to lend a hand or bring your hand to bear on the work going on. *Bears* refer to those who are helping.

belaying pin: a large wooden or metal pin that fits into a hole in a rail on a ship or boat, and to which a rope can be fastened.

Black Ensign: pirates' flag; the flag traditionally flown by a pirate ship, depicting a white skull and crossbones against a black background. Also known as the Jolly Roger.

blackguard: a man who behaves in a dishonorable or contemptible way.

bluejackets: sailors.

bone in her teeth: said of a ship speeding along throwing up spray or foam under the bow.

Boney: a nickname, often what the British called Napoleon Bonaparte, the name being both short and displaying a certain lack of respect.

bow chasers: a pair of long guns mounted forward in the bow of a sailing warship to fire directly ahead; used when chasing an enemy to shoot away her sails and rigging.

broadside: all the guns that can be fired from one side of a warship or their simultaneous fire in naval warfare.

bulwark: a solid wall enclosing the perimeter of a weather or main deck for the protection of persons or objects on deck.

butt: 1. an object of ridicule or contempt. 2. a remaining part.

cable length: a maritime unit of length measuring 720 feet (220 meters) in the US and 608 feet (185 meters) in England.

canister: a metallic cylinder packed with small cast-iron balls that scatter upon discharge from a cannon.

cat: cat-o'-nine-tails; a whip, usually having nine knotted lines or cords fastened to a handle, used for flogging.

Coast Range: a series of mountain ranges along the Pacific coast of North America, extending from lower California to southeast Alaska.

cockade: a rosette, knot of ribbon, etc., usually worn on the hat as part of a uniform, as a badge of office or the like.

cockleshell: a light flimsy boat.

111

cockpit: a cabin on the lower deck of a man-o'-war where the wounded in battle were tended.

Continental Alliance: also called the First Coalition, an alliance formed between Prussia, Austria, Spain and Great Britain (1792–1797) after the French Revolution (1789) in an effort to overthrow the revolutionary government of France and restore the rule of the French monarchy. By the end of 1797, this alliance had collapsed following Napoleon's victories in Prussia and Austria and a separate peace treaty was negotiated with Spain, leaving only Britain in the field fighting against France.

corselet: part of a diver's suit consisting of a breastplate made of copper or iron, shaped so that it fits comfortably over the shoulders, chest and back. Once in place, the corselet is bolted to the suit and the diving helmet is then locked onto the corselet.

coxswained: acted or served as a coxswain for; steered the ship's boat and been in charge of its crew.

crosstrees: a pair of horizontal rods attached to a sailing ship's mast to spread the rigging, especially at the head of a topmast.

de Brueys: Vice Admiral Francois-Paul Brueys d'Aigalliers, Count de Brueys (1753–1798); French commander in the Battle of the Nile, in which the French Revolutionary Navy was defeated by the British under Admiral Nelson at Aboukir Bay on August 2, 1798.

diving lung: Submarine Escape Lung; device developed and tested by Admiral Charles Momsen of the US Navy between 1929 and 1932 for the purpose of rescuing sailors trapped in submarines. Also called the "Momsen Lung," it consisted of an oblong rubber bag that recycled exhaled air to provide oxygen for sailors to ascend to the surface of the water.

diving rudder: one of the movable plane surfaces attached to the hull of a submarine, that controls the vertical motion.

eighties: naval vessels carrying eighty guns.

fathom: a unit of length equal to six feet (1.83 meters), used in measuring the depth of water.

flag captain: captain of the flagship, the ship used by the commanding officer of a group of naval ships.

flarebacks: flames produced in the breeches of guns by ignition of residual gases.

frigates: fast naval vessels of the late eighteenth and early nineteenth centuries, heavily armed on one or two decks.

galleon: a large three-masted sailing ship, usually with two or more decks; used mainly by the Spanish from the fifteenth to eighteenth centuries for war and commerce.

gangway: a narrow, movable platform or ramp forming a bridge by which to board or leave a ship.

gay: impertinent and forward.

Gibbs Light: Gibbs Hill Lighthouse; it is the taller of two lighthouses on Bermuda, and the first of only a few lighthouses in the world to be made of cast iron. While it is not extremely tall by lighthouse standards, the hill that it stands on is one of the highest on the island. First lit in 1846 with kerosene burners, it is now automated to run on electricity.

gig: a boat reserved for the use of the captain of a ship.

girded the loins: braced for vigorous action or energetic endurance.

G-men: government men; agents of the Federal Bureau of Investigation.

grape: a cluster of small cast-iron balls formerly used as a charge for a cannon.

grappling hooks: composite hooks attached to ropes designed to be thrown or projected a distance so that the hooks will engage with the target.

gun captain: a petty officer in command of a gun crew on a ship.

gunwale: the upper edge of the side of a boat. Originally a gunwale was a platform where guns were mounted, and was designed to accommodate the additional stresses imposed by the artillery being used.

halyard: a rope used for raising and lowering a sail.

hawse: hawse pipe; iron or steel pipe in the stem or bow of a vessel, through which an anchor cable passes.

hawsers: cables or ropes used in mooring or towing ships.

heeled: inclined to one side; tilted.

HMS: His Majesty's Ship.

inboard: within the hull or toward the center of a vessel.

Jacob's ladder: a hanging ladder having ropes or chains supporting wooden or metal rungs or steps.

jolly boat: a light boat carried at the stern of a sailing vessel.

keel: a lengthwise structure along the base of a ship, and in some vessels extended downwards as a ridge to increase stability.

langrage: shot used in naval warfare consisting of a case filled with fragments of iron for tearing the sails and rigging of enemy ships.

liners: ships of the line; sailing warships large enough to be in the line of battle.

man-o'-war: any armed ship of a national navy, usually carrying between 20 and 120 guns.

marcel: a hairstyle characterized by deep, continuous waves.

marlinespike: a tool made from wood or metal, and used in rope work for tasks such as untwisting rope for splicing or untying knots that tighten up under tension. It is basically a polished cone tapered to a rounded point, usually six to twelve inches long, although sometimes it is longer.

midshipman: a student naval officer educated principally at sea.

mizzen: a fore-and-aft sail set on the mizzenmast, the third mast from forward in a vessel having three or more masts.

Napoleonic Wars: a series of intermittent wars fought between France, led by Napoleon Bonaparte, and a number of European nations, principally Great Britain, Prussia, Austria and Russia (1796–1815). The wars ended with Napoleon's final defeat at the Battle of Waterloo at the hands of Prussian and British forces.

Nelson: Viscount Horatio Nelson (1758–1805), British admiral famous for his participation in the Napoleonic Wars. He was noted for his considerable ability to inspire and bring out the best in his men, to the point that it gained the name "The Nelson Touch." He was revered as few military figures have been throughout British history.

Newton: Sir Isaac Newton (1643–1727); English mathematician and physicist. Famous for his laws of motion, which are laws concerning the relations between force, motion, acceleration, mass and inertia, and that govern the motion of material objects.

'Od's wounds: by God's wounds; used as an exclamation.

paint the town: to party; to go out and enjoy yourself in the evening, often drinking alcohol and dancing.

pigboat: a submarine.

Pitt: William Pitt the Younger (1759–1806); the English statesman who prepared England for war against Napoleonic France.

points: a point is 11.25 degrees on a compass. Sailing within two points of a breeze refers to sailing within 22.50 degrees of the direction of the wind.

powder monkeys: boys employed on warships to carry gunpowder from the magazine to the guns.

press gang: a body of persons under the command of an officer, formerly employed to impress others for service, especially in the navy or army.

press ganging: forcing (a person) into military or naval service.

put in: to enter a port or harbor, especially for shelter, repairs or provisions.

pylon: a tower marking a turning point in a race among aircraft.

quarterdeck: the rear part of the upper deck of a ship, usually reserved for officers.

rag: a sail or any piece of canvas.

ratline: a small rope fastened horizontally between the shrouds in the rigging of a sailing ship to form a rung of a ladder for the crew going aloft.

Scheherazade: the female narrator of *The Arabian Nights*, who during one thousand and one adventurous nights saved her life by entertaining her husband, the king, with stories.

schooner: a fast sailing ship with at least two masts and with sails set lengthwise.

scow: an old or clumsy boat; hulk; tub.

scuppers: openings in the side of a ship at deck level that allow water to run off.

scuttle: to sink a ship deliberately by opening seacocks or making openings in the bottom.

seacocks: valves below the waterline in a ship's hull, used for admitting outside water into some part of the hull.

seventy-fours: naval vessels carrying seventy-four guns.

shrouds: supporting ropes or wires that extend down from the top of a mast.

sirrah: a term of address used to inferiors or children to express impatience, contempt, etc.

son of Neptune: a sailor who has crossed the equator.

Spanish Plate Fleet: Spanish treasure fleets; along with gold, silver, gems and other trade goods, the ships were filled with rare Chinese porcelain tableware, hence the name "Plate Fleet."

spanker: a sail set from the aftermost lower mast of a sailing ship.

spars: strong poles, especially those used as masts to support the sails on ships.

St. Kitts and Nevis: a two-island country in the West Indies, east-southeast of Puerto Rico, it is the smallest nation in the Americas in both area and population. Formerly a British colony, the islands gained independence in 1983. A narrow strait separates the two islands, which are volcanic in origin and mountainous with heavy vegetation. The chief settlement on Nevis is Charlestown.

Syracuse: capital city and port of Syracuse Province, Sicily.

tar: a sailor.

Toulon: city in southern France and a large military harbor on the Mediterranean coast.

trades or **trade winds:** any of the nearly constant easterly winds that dominate most of the tropics and subtropics throughout the world, blowing mainly from the northeast in the Northern Hemisphere, and from the southeast in the Southern Hemisphere.

trajectory: the path that a projectile makes through space under the action of given forces such as thrust, wind and gravity.

tramp: a freight vessel that does not run regularly between fixed ports, but takes a cargo wherever shippers desire.

transom: a small rectangular window above a door.

tricolor: the French national flag, consisting of three equal vertical bands of blue, white and red.

'tween decks: between decks; spaces between two continuous decks in the hull of a vessel.

under weigh: in motion; underway.

unstepped: a mast that has been removed from its step, the block in which the heel of the mast is fixed.

wandering Jew: any of various trailing or creeping plants having leaves that are green or varied in color; a popular houseplant.

warp: to move (a vessel) into a desired place or position by hauling on a rope that has been fastened to something fixed, as a dock or anchored buoy.

ways: timber frameworks on which a ship is built, and along which it slides when launching.

weigh anchor: take up the anchor when ready to sail.

West Indies: a group of islands in the North Atlantic between North and South America, comprising the Greater Antilles, the Lesser Antilles and the Bahamas.

wharf rat: someone who lives near wharves and lives by pilfering from ships or warehouses.

whelp: a youth, especially an impudent or despised one.

yard: a long rod, mounted crosswise on a mast and tapering toward the ends, that supports and spreads a sail.

FULL-RIGGED SAILING SHIP

1: flying jib
2: jib
3: fore-topmast staysail
4: foresail
5: lower fore-topsail
6: upper fore-topsail
7: fore-topgallant sail
8: fore-royal
9: fore-skysail
10: lower studding sail
(never on the main)
11: fore-topmast studding sail
12: fore-topgallant studding sail
13: fore-royal studding sail
14: main staysail
15: main-topmast staysail
16: main-topgallant staysail
17: main-royal staysail
18: mainsail

19: lower main topsail
20: upper main topsail
21: main-topgallant sail
22: main royal
23: main skysail
24: main-topmast studding sail
25: main-topgallant studding sail
26: main-royal studding sail
27: mizzen staysail
28: mizzen-topmast staysail
29: mizzen-topgallant staysail
30: mizzen-royal staysail
31: mizzen sail (crossjack)
32: lower mizzen topsail
33: upper mizzen topsail
34: mizzen-topgallant sail
35: mizzen royal
36: mizzen skysail
37: spanker

L. Ron Hubbard
in the Golden Age
of Pulp Fiction

*In writing an adventure story
a writer has to know that he is adventuring
for a lot of people who cannot.
The writer has to take them here and there
about the globe and show them
excitement and love and realism.
As long as that writer is living the part of an
adventurer when he is hammering
the keys, he is succeeding with his story.*

*Adventuring is a state of mind.
If you adventure through life, you have a
good chance to be a success on paper.*

*Adventure doesn't mean globe-trotting,
exactly, and it doesn't mean great deeds.
Adventuring is like art.
You have to live it to make it real.*

—*L. RON HUBBARD*

L. Ron Hubbard
and American
Pulp Fiction

B ORN March 13, 1911, L. Ron Hubbard lived a life at least as expansive as the stories with which he enthralled a hundred million readers through a fifty-year career.

Originally hailing from Tilden, Nebraska, he spent his formative years in a classically rugged Montana, replete with the cowpunchers, lawmen and desperadoes who would later people his Wild West adventures. And lest anyone imagine those adventures were drawn from vicarious experience, he was not only breaking broncs at a tender age, he was also among the few whites ever admitted into Blackfoot society as a bona fide blood brother. While if only to round out an otherwise rough and tumble youth, his mother was that rarity of her time—a thoroughly educated woman—who introduced her son to the classics of Occidental literature even before his seventh birthday.

But as any dedicated L. Ron Hubbard reader will attest, his world extended far beyond Montana. In point of fact, and as the son of a United States naval officer, by the age of eighteen he had traveled over a quarter of a million miles. Included therein were three Pacific crossings to a then still mysterious Asia, where he ran with the likes of Her British Majesty's agent-in-place

L. Ron Hubbard,
left, at Congressional
Airport, Washington,
DC, 1931, with
members of George
Washington
University flying
club.

for North China, and the last in the line of Royal Magicians from the court of Kublai Khan. For the record, L. Ron Hubbard was also among the first Westerners to gain admittance to forbidden Tibetan monasteries below Manchuria, and his photographs of China's Great Wall long graced American geography texts.

Upon his return to the United States and a hasty completion of his interrupted high school education, the young Ron Hubbard entered George Washington University. There, as fans of his aerial adventures may have heard, he earned his wings as a pioneering barnstormer at the dawn of American aviation. He also earned a place in free-flight record books for the longest sustained flight above Chicago. Moreover, as a roving reporter for *Sportsman Pilot* (featuring his first professionally penned articles), he further helped inspire a generation of pilots who would take America to world airpower.

Immediately beyond his sophomore year, Ron embarked on the first of his famed ethnological expeditions, initially to then untrammeled Caribbean shores (descriptions of which would later fill a whole series of West Indies mystery-thrillers). That the Puerto Rican interior would also figure into the future of Ron Hubbard stories was likewise no accident. For in addition to cultural studies of the island, a 1932–33

LRH expedition is rightly remembered as conducting the first complete mineralogical survey of a Puerto Rico under United States jurisdiction.

There was many another adventure along this vein: As a lifetime member of the famed Explorers Club, L. Ron Hubbard charted North Pacific waters with the first shipboard radio direction finder, and so pioneered a long-range navigation system universally employed until the late twentieth century. While not to put too fine an edge on it, he also held a rare Master Mariner's license to pilot any vessel, of any tonnage in any ocean.

Yet lest we stray too far afield, there is an LRH note at this juncture in his saga, and it reads in part:

"I started out writing for the pulps, writing the best I knew, writing for every mag on the stands, slanting as well as I could."

Capt. L. Ron Hubbard in Ketchikan, Alaska, 1940, on his Alaskan Radio Experimental Expedition, the first of three voyages conducted under the Explorers Club flag.

To which one might add: His earliest submissions date from the summer of 1934, and included tales drawn from true-to-life Asian adventures, with characters roughly modeled on British/American intelligence operatives he had known in Shanghai. His early Westerns were similarly peppered with details drawn from personal experience. Although therein lay a first hard lesson from the often cruel world of the pulps. His first Westerns were soundly rejected as lacking the authenticity of a Max Brand yarn (a particularly frustrating comment given L. Ron Hubbard's Westerns came straight from his Montana homeland, while Max Brand was a mediocre New York poet named Frederick Schiller Faust, who turned out implausible six-shooter tales from the terrace of an Italian villa).

Nevertheless, and needless to say, L. Ron Hubbard persevered and soon earned a reputation as among the most publishable names in pulp fiction, with a ninety percent placement rate of first-draft manuscripts. He was also among the most prolific, averaging between seventy and a hundred thousand words a month. Hence the rumors that L. Ron Hubbard had redesigned a typewriter for faster keyboard action and pounded out manuscripts on a continuous roll of butcher paper to save the precious seconds it took to insert a single sheet of paper into manual typewriters of the day.

That all L. Ron Hubbard stories did not run beneath said byline is yet another aspect of pulp fiction lore. That is, as publishers periodically rejected manuscripts from top-drawer authors if only to avoid paying top dollar, L. Ron Hubbard and company just as frequently replied with submissions under various pseudonyms. In Ron's case, the list

A MAN OF MANY NAMES

Between 1934 and 1950, L. Ron Hubbard authored more than fifteen million words of fiction in more than two hundred classic publications. To supply his fans and editors with stories across an array of genres and pulp titles, he adopted fifteen pseudonyms in addition to his already renowned L. Ron Hubbard byline.

Winchester Remington Colt
Lt. Jonathan Daly
Capt. Charles Gordon
Capt. L. Ron Hubbard
Bernard Hubbel
Michael Keith
Rene Lafayette
Legionnaire 148
Legionnaire 14830
Ken Martin
Scott Morgan
Lt. Scott Morgan
Kurt von Rachen
Barry Randolph
Capt. Humbert Reynolds

126

included: Rene Lafayette, Captain
Charles Gordon, Lt. Scott Morgan
and the notorious Kurt von
Rachen—supposedly on the lam
for a murder rap, while hammering
out two-fisted prose in Argentina.
The point: While L. Ron Hubbard
as Ken Martin spun stories of
Southeast Asian intrigue, LRH as
Barry Randolph authored tales of

romance on the Western range—which, stretching
between a dozen genres is how he came to stand
among the two hundred elite authors providing
close to a million tales through the glory days of
American Pulp Fiction.

*L. Ron Hubbard,
circa 1930, at the
outset of a literary
career that would
finally span half a
century.*

In evidence of exactly that, by 1936 L. Ron Hubbard was
literally leading pulp fiction's elite as president of New York's
American Fiction Guild. Members included a veritable
pulp hall of fame: Lester "Doc Savage" Dent, Walter "The
Shadow" Gibson, and the legendary Dashiell Hammett—to
cite but a few.

Also in evidence of just where L. Ron Hubbard stood
within his first two years on the American pulp circuit: By the
spring of 1937, he was ensconced in Hollywood, adopting a
Caribbean thriller for Columbia Pictures, remembered today as
The Secret of Treasure Island. Comprising fifteen thirty-minute
episodes, the L. Ron Hubbard screenplay led to the most
profitable matinée serial in Hollywood history. In accord
with Hollywood culture, he was thereafter continually called

The 1937 Secret of Treasure Island, *a fifteen-episode serial adapted for the screen by L. Ron Hubbard from his novel,* Murder at Pirate Castle.

upon to rewrite/doctor scripts—most famously for long-time friend and fellow adventurer Clark Gable.

In the interim—and herein lies another distinctive chapter of the L. Ron Hubbard story—he continually worked to open Pulp Kingdom gates to up-and-coming authors. Or, for that matter, anyone who wished to write. It was a fairly unconventional stance, as markets were already thin and competition razor sharp. But the fact remains, it was an L. Ron Hubbard hallmark that he vehemently lobbied on behalf of young authors—regularly supplying instructional articles to trade journals, guest-lecturing to short story classes at George Washington University and Harvard, and even founding his own creative writing competition. It was established in 1940, dubbed the Golden Pen, and guaranteed winners both New York representation and publication in *Argosy.*

But it was John W. Campbell Jr.'s *Astounding Science Fiction* that finally proved the most memorable LRH vehicle. While every fan of L. Ron Hubbard's galactic epics undoubtedly knows the story, it nonetheless bears repeating: By late 1938, the pulp publishing magnate of Street & Smith was determined to revamp *Astounding Science Fiction* for broader readership. In particular, senior editorial director F. Orlin Tremaine called for stories with a stronger *human element.* When acting editor John W. Campbell balked, preferring his spaceship-driven tales,

Tremaine enlisted Hubbard. Hubbard, in turn, replied with the genre's first truly *character-driven* works, wherein heroes are pitted not against bug-eyed monsters but the mystery and majesty of deep space itself—and thus was launched the Golden Age of Science Fiction.

The names alone are enough to quicken the pulse of any science fiction aficionado, including LRH friend and protégé, Robert Heinlein, Isaac Asimov, A. E. van Vogt and Ray Bradbury. Moreover, when coupled with LRH stories of fantasy, we further come to what's rightly been described as the foundation of every modern tale of horror: L. Ron Hubbard's immortal *Fear*. It was rightly proclaimed by Stephen King as one of the very few works to genuinely warrant that overworked term "classic"—as in: *"This is a classic tale of creeping, surreal menace and horror. . . . This is one of the really, really good ones."*

L. Ron Hubbard, 1948, among fellow science fiction luminaries at the World Science Fiction Convention in Toronto.

To accommodate the greater body of L. Ron Hubbard fantasies, Street & Smith inaugurated *Unknown*—a classic pulp if there ever was one, and wherein readers were soon thrilling to the likes of *Typewriter in the Sky* and *Slaves of Sleep* of which Frederik Pohl would declare: *"There are bits and pieces from Ron's work that became part of the language in ways that very few other writers managed."*

And, indeed, at J. W. Campbell Jr.'s insistence, Ron was regularly drawing on themes from the Arabian Nights and so introducing readers to a world of genies, jinn, Aladdin and Sinbad—all of which, of course, continue to float through cultural mythology to this day.

At least as influential in terms of post-apocalypse stories was L. Ron Hubbard's 1940 *Final Blackout*. Generally acclaimed as the finest anti-war novel of the decade and among the ten best works of the genre ever authored—here, too, was a tale that would live on in ways few other writers

imagined. Hence, the later Robert Heinlein verdict: "Final Blackout *is as perfect a piece of science fiction as has ever been written.*"

Like many another who both lived and wrote American pulp adventure, the war proved a tragic end to Ron's sojourn in the pulps. He served with distinction in four theaters and was highly decorated

Portland, Oregon, 1943; L. Ron Hubbard captain of the US Navy subchaser PC 815.

for commanding corvettes in the North Pacific. He was also grievously wounded in combat, lost many a close friend and colleague and thus resolved to say farewell to pulp fiction and devote himself to what it had supported these many years—namely, his serious research.

But in no way was the LRH literary saga at an end, for as he wrote some thirty years later, in 1980:

"Recently there came a period when I had little to do. This was novel in a life so crammed with busy years, and I decided to amuse myself by writing a novel that was pure science fiction."

That work was *Battlefield Earth: A Saga of the Year 3000*. It was an immediate *New York Times* bestseller and, in fact, the first international science fiction blockbuster in decades. It was not, however, L. Ron Hubbard's magnum opus, as that distinction is generally reserved for his next and final work: The 1.2 million word *Mission Earth*.

> **Final Blackout**
> *is as perfect a piece of science fiction as has ever been written.*
>
> —Robert Heinlein

How he managed those 1.2 million words in just over twelve months is yet another piece of the L. Ron Hubbard legend. But the fact remains, he did indeed author a ten-volume *dekalogy* that lives in publishing history for the fact that each and every volume of the series was also a *New York Times* bestseller.

Moreover, as subsequent generations discovered L. Ron Hubbard through republished works and novelizations of his screenplays, the mere fact of his name on a cover signaled an international bestseller. . . . Until, to date, sales of his works exceed hundreds of millions, and he otherwise remains among the most enduring and widely read authors in literary history. Although as a final word on the tales of L. Ron Hubbard, perhaps it's enough to simply reiterate what editors told readers in the glory days of American Pulp Fiction:

He writes the way he does, brothers, because he's been there, seen it and done it!

THE STORIES FROM THE GOLDEN AGE

Your ticket to adventure starts here with the Stories from
the Golden Age collection by master storyteller L. Ron Hubbard.
These gripping tales are set in a kaleidoscope of exotic locales and brim
with fascinating characters, including some of the
most vile villains, dangerous dames and brazen heroes
you'll ever get to meet.

The entire collection of over one hundred and fifty stories is being
released in a series of eighty books and audiobooks.
For an up-to-date listing of available titles,
go to www.goldenagestories.com.

AIR ADVENTURE

Arctic Wings	*Man-Killers of the Air*
The Battling Pilot	*On Blazing Wings*
Boomerang Bomber	*Red Death Over China*
The Crate Killer	*Sabotage in the Sky*
The Dive Bomber	*Sky Birds Dare!*
Forbidden Gold	*The Sky-Crasher*
Hurtling Wings	*Trouble on His Wings*
The Lieutenant Takes the Sky	*Wings Over Ethiopia*

FAR-FLUNG ADVENTURE

The Adventure of "X"   *Hurricane*
All Frontiers Are Jealous   *The Iron Duke*
The Barbarians   *Machine Gun 21,000*
The Black Sultan   *Medals for Mahoney*
Black Towers to Danger   *Price of a Hat*
The Bold Dare All   *Red Sand*
Buckley Plays a Hunch   *The Sky Devil*
The Cossack   *The Small Boss of Nunaloha*
Destiny's Drum   *The Squad That Never Came Back*
Escape for Three   *Starch and Stripes*
Fifty-Fifty O'Brien   *Tomb of the Ten Thousand Dead*
The Headhunters   *Trick Soldier*
Hell's Legionnaire   *While Bugles Blow!*
He Walked to War   *Yukon Madness*
Hostage to Death

SEA ADVENTURE

Cargo of Coffins   *The Phantom Patrol*
The Drowned City   *Sea Fangs*
False Cargo   *Submarine*
Grounded   *Twenty Fathoms Down*
Loot of the Shanung   *Under the Black Ensign*
Mister Tidwell, Gunner

TALES FROM THE ORIENT

MYSTERY

135

FANTASY

Borrowed Glory   If I Were You
The Crossroads   The Last Drop
Danger in the Dark   The Room
The Devil's Rescue   The Tramp
He Didn't Like Cats

SCIENCE FICTION

The Automagic Horse   A Matter of Matter
Battle of Wizards   The Obsolete Weapon
Battling Bolto   One Was Stubborn
The Beast   The Planet Makers
Beyond All Weapons   The Professor Was a Thief
A Can of Vacuum   The Slaver
The Conroy Diary   Space Can
The Dangerous Dimension   Strain
Final Enemy   Tough Old Man
The Great Secret   240,000 Miles Straight Up
Greed   When Shadows Fall
The Invaders

WESTERN

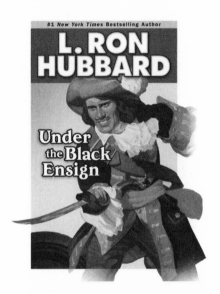

JOIN THE PULP REVIVAL
America in the 1930s and 40s

Pulp fiction was in its heyday and 30 million readers were regularly riveted by the larger-than-life tales of master storyteller L. Ron Hubbard. For this was pulp fiction's golden age, when the writing was raw and every page packed a walloping punch.

That magic can now be yours. An evocative world of nefarious villains, exotic intrigues, courageous heroes and heroines—a world that today's cinema has barely tapped for tales of adventure and swashbucklers.

Enroll today in the Stories from the Golden Age Club and begin receiving your monthly feature edition selected from more than 150 stories in the collection.

You may choose to enjoy them as either a paperback or audiobook for the special membership price of $9.95 each month along with FREE shipping and handling.